MW01128958

JACK OF SPADES

A MAFIA ROMANCE

RENEE ROSE

ACKNOWLEDGEMENTS

Thank you so much for picking up my mafia romance. If you enjoy it, I would so appreciate your review—they make a huge difference for indie authors.

My enormous gratitude to Aubrey Cara for her beta read and for Maggie Ryan's rush job on editing. I love you guys!

Thanks also to the amazing members of my Facebook group, Renee's Romper Room. If you're not a part of it, you should be—the kink talk and support inspire me every day!

JACK OF SPADES

Jack of Spades: A Mafia Romance
Vegas Underground, Book Two

by Renee Rose

"YOU'RE AT MY MERCY NOW, *AMORE.*"

Sorry, *bella.* You got dealt the losing hand.
Witness to a crime, you're my prisoner now.
I didn't mean for things to happen this way,
But tying you to my bed and making you scream
is an unexpected pleasure. A privilege, really.
And even if I did trust you, now that I've had a taste,
I'm not sure I'd let you go…

orey

THREE KINDS of gamblers spend big at my roulette table.

There's the guy who's all up in his head. He's quiet, body language closed. He sits with hunched shoulders and barely meets my eye. He plays odds, usually has a system he sticks to religiously. Like he always plays red and doubles his bet when he loses.

Then there's the reckless gambler. He's riding emotion, drugs or alcohol. He's the opposite of the first kind. No system, totally haphazard. He might ask the woman beside him for her favorite number and bet it.

Then, there's the gut gambler, my personal favorite. He carries an electricity with him that often carries the entire table away. It's the guy who's found the magic. Lady Luck, mojo, their stars aligning—who knows what it is, but they have an energy they're following. They stay in the flow, following their intuition and bet right every time.

Often they appear similar to reckless gamblers: they're outgoing, social. They engage with the people around them, including me, their croupier.

The whale—that's Vegas for big spender—at my table tonight is neither reckless, nor a gut gambler, although he has the personality and style of both. He's gorgeous with a finely tailored suit and European flair, like he stepped off the pages of an Italian men's magazine. He flirts shamelessly with me and chats up the people around him.

I scoop and stack the chips and award the winnings with practiced finesse, doing a one-handed split and stack and moving with lightning speed.

"There she goes, beauty and talent."

It's cheesy, but I flash him a smile. I like having him at my table, love his charm and flair, the big tips, yet my spidey sense keeps sounding. There's something off about him.

He's down two thousand at the moment. He slides his chips out onto the table at the last minute, right as I wave my hand and call no more bets. He sets them up sloppily, too. I can't tell if he wants them in the box for *Third Twelve* or *Odd*.

"Which one, sir?" I lean forward to get his attention as the wheel spins.

He's been drinking quite a bit, but he doesn't appear intoxicated. His eyes flick to my cleavage—which I still manage to work despite the masculine uniform—then back to my face before he gives me a slow, good-natured grin. "Odds, please. Sorry for that."

"No slop," I warn, and scoot the chips over as the ball settles.

He wins. He slides two hundred-dollar chips across the table to me as a tip. When I pull his chips in, I see he's embedded a ten dollar chip in the middle instead of a hundred. I flick my gaze up and see he's watching me. He winks.

Asshole.

I subtly signal for Security to come over.

It's not the first time I've been propositioned to cheat for a customer. It happens often enough. It sort of boggles my mind that he'd spend two hundred bucks paying me off to make ninety. But I suppose it was a test. Once he found out if I'd give him anything, he would've tried it again and again.

Vincent, the security manager on the floor tonight ambles over and stands close to me, dipping his head to listen.

"This guy's playing slop and trying to slip low chips in his stack."

Later, I would realize Vincent seemed a little too pleased with me, but it doesn't register. I'm just ignoring the flutters in my belly as he walks around to escort the dude out. I'm not sorry. I did the right thing, for sure. I'm only disappointed because the guy was attractive and sort of fascinating to me, and I'd fantasized for just a moment about him asking me out.

But whatever. I'm not going to risk this job, not even for a sexy man in a sharp suit. Working at the Bellissimo

RENEE ROSE

is like a job, education and socialization all rolled into one glamorous package. It's owned by the notorious Nico Tacone, of the Tacone Chicago crime family, who rules the place with an iron fist. I wouldn't fuck with him. Even if he is in love with my cousin.

I finish my shift and head toward the employee locker rooms. When I pass the hallway toward the security offices, I stop short.

Vincent is standing in a relaxed posture, shooting the shit with none other than the sexy suit from my table.

"Corey," he grins and beckons me closer. "Come here, I want to introduce you to someone."

Oh Jesus. He was a secret shopper. Or whatever you call a security test. I don't know why it pisses me off, but it does. My stomach tightens up into a knot as I stride over.

"Corey, meet Stefano Tacone, our new Head of Security."

I lift my hand to slap Stefano's face. I don't know why I do it. Yes, I have a redhead's temper and I grew up in a violent family. Still, I should know better.

He catches my wrist and uses it to pull me right up against him. "I wouldn't." His warning is less a growl than a low, smoky rumble. Like he's dirty-talking me right here in the hallway.

My body responds immediately, my core turning molten. Of course, my damn cheeks heat, too. And believe me, on a redhead, there's no mistaking a blush.

"No one strikes a Tacone without regretting it." It's a threat, yet it's still spoken good-naturedly, with the same

4

heart-stopping charm he used out on the floor, trying to get me to cheat for him.

Shit. Did I actually just lift a hand to a mob boss? A chill slithers down my back.

I'm so going to lose my job.

Except Stefano doesn't look angry. He looks like he wants to eat me for lunch.

I figure my best bet is to own my mistake. "Forgive me."

Stefano

THE BEAUTY IN MY ARMS—WELL, not quite in my arms, more at my mercy—meets my gaze with courage.

I see neither fear nor defiance in the bright blue eyes, merely bald curiosity, almost a hint of fascination.

Likewise, bella.

I picked her table for a reason, and it wasn't because anyone suspected her of cheating. Quite the opposite. The floor manager says she always attracts a crowd of gentlemen, earns big tips. She's fast and showy, exuding just the right balance of cool professional and warm invitation in any game she deals. I tested her because we need a dealer for private games upstairs.

Now, though, I want to play all kinds of private games with her and none of them involve a deck of cards or a roulette wheel.

"I don't like being humiliated," she says. For a moment,

I think she's speaking to my thoughts, and then I realize it's her justification for trying to slap me. She turns her wrist in my hand, attempting to get free.

I don't allow it, pulling her small hand up to my mouth to brush my lips across her knuckles. "I'll remember that," I murmur.

She goes still, throat working on a swallow. She's so close I sense the heat of her lanky body, notice the slight tremble in her fingers, despite the evenness of her gaze.

There goes the blush again, giving her away. I want to keep holding her tight against my body, watching those electric blue eyes dilate every time I speak, but if I do, I'll end up shoving her against the wall and having my way with the tits she wields like weapons.

No other female croupier looks like this one. The new uniform is a white oxford, crimson vest, and a bow tie, for God's sake.

Corey manages to make the outfit sinful, though. The short black skirt hugs every curve of her ass, hips and waist, setting off a pair of long slender legs. She has the blouse unbuttoned and open to the vest, the bow tie worn on the inside like a lover's collar. How I'd love to put a collar and leash on this beautiful creature and bring her to heel; she'd take some training, too. The *coupe de grace* of the outfit is her vest. She chose one two sizes too small, making it appear more like a bustier or corset, cinching below her breasts and pushing them in and up until they're begging to spill from her blouse. I can't tell with the vest if her nipples are hard, but judging from her parted lips and short breath, I'd guess they are.

I know I sprouted a chub just from getting rough with

her. Which would probably be a good reason to let her go. I force a little self-control and release her.

"Come into my office, let's have a little chat." I wave my arm to indicate my new office.

Again, she holds her head high, tossing her long thick waves over her shoulder as she precedes me to the closed door.

She waits for me to open it, presumably because it's my office, but I take distinct satisfaction in reaching past her to hold it open, like we're on some kind of classy date instead of interview.

"Have a seat, Corey."

She shoots me a wary glance as she takes a seat opposite me at my desk. "Did Nico sic you on me?"

I arch a brow. "You're on a first-name basis with my brother?"

"Mr. Tacone," she amends with a slight flush. I love her blushes because they are so at odds with her natural confidence. "No, sorry, not at all. He's dating my cousin, so I just—"

"Ah, yes. *The woman.* The reason Nico called me back from Sicily."

Corey appears taken aback. "What do you mean?"

I wink. "I'm here because he was in danger of losing her—working too many hours. I haven't met her yet, this cousin of yours." I let my gaze travel across Corey's face, down to her enticing cleavage and back. "I can see why he might be enchanted."

No blush this time. In fact, I think she suppressed an eye roll. I really do like this girl. Taming her would be so fun.

"What's her name?"

She crosses her long legs, ease creeping into her posture. "Sondra. And you probably won't meet her. She's gone."

I knew this already. It's a good thing I arrived when I did because Nico's been completely off the rails since his woman walked out on him. I have yet to see the guy, but I know he's flown home to Chicago to figure out his arranged marriage and other shit with our father.

She tries to take back the lead in the conversation, "So why target me? I'm a good dealer. I keep my nose clean."

My lips twitch. I love her spirit. She's going to be perfect for upstairs. I'll just have to make sure no one touches her because I'm already starting to feel a bit proprietary over the looker. "Your supervisors like you, yes. The ones who aren't jealous." I noticed the female supervisor gave her much lower marks than the males.

The corner of Corey's lips tug up. I like the easy recognition she gives to my statement. She already has correctly interpreted my words and isn't bothered by them. I've already made up my mind—she's smart. Confident. Easy on the eyes. She's perfect.

"We're switching you to higher stakes games. Private ones." I'm not asking; I'm telling. This is the way Tacones do business.

Now I caught her off-guard. Her crimson lips part, and for a moment, no sound comes out. "That sounds dangerous." Her voice strangles slightly on the last word.

I raise a brow, both curious and impressed by her conclusion. "It's not. I'll be there for every game. I won't let anything happen to you." When she remains still, I say, "Or is it me you're worried about?"

Slight blush tells me she's definitely interested, but she shakes her head. "No. Yes. I guess I mean it sounds... illegal."

There it is. I so appreciate people who can be direct.

I spread my hands. "This is Las Vegas. We have a gambling license. It's the reason my brother moved here."

"Right. Of course." She nods, averting her eyes. I fucking love those little signs of submission on an otherwise alpha female. Like when she apologized for trying to slap me. She knows when to hold her own and when to roll over. It makes me want to flex my dominance in all kinds of filthy ways—put her on her knees and choke her with my cock. Tie her to my bed and keep her screaming all night long. Win her obedience with a whip and a carrot.

She doesn't believe me, which again, shows she's smart. Gambling may not be illegal, but there are all sorts of sordid, underground things that happen around the fringe. Like the sometimes forcible collection of unusual bets placed by desperate men.

This is the game my brother Nico learned from *La Famiglia*. He was a genius to bring it to Vegas, where much of it is legal. Yeah, it means he pays taxes, but believe me, not as much as he should.

"It won't be all the time. Three or four nights a week. We'll double your base pay and the tips should increase, too."

"You're not giving me a choice." It's a statement, not a question.

9

I wink. "You noticed that, did you? I need you in the upstairs games, Corey. End of story."

Anger flickers in her expression but she quickly hides it. "Why me?"

I lift my shoulders in a casual shrug. "You're professional. Cool and reserved. Trustworthy. Beautiful. In short, you're exactly what I'm looking for."

The wariness in her gaze becomes more apparent. Her dislike of my offer shows on her face, but she says, "Well. I guess I don't have a say in the matter."

I'm slightly surprised. I knew she wasn't a bimbo who'd fall all over herself, flattered, but I don't think I'm giving her a bad deal. And if her cousin's already in bed with Nico—literally—I can't think she has major hangups about our family.

But maybe she does.

"Oh there's always a choice, Ms. Simonson. You can walk out that door."

Eh, I may be the young charming one, but can be as much of a *stronzo* as any of my brothers. Maybe more.

Her dark painted lips compress. "I'm not doing that, Mr. Tacone." Her blue eyes blaze when she meets the challenge in my gaze.

"Good." I stand up and hold out my hand. "Welcome to the big time."

She stands and I note her brief hesitation before taking my hand, but I give her a warm smile as we shake.

"Tomorrow night. Be here by eight."

"Yes, sir. Here—your office?"

I nod, even though it's a terrible idea. I should foist her onto Sal or Leo, tell her somewhere else to meet, but I can't turn down the idea of having her here, in my space. My personal croupier. "Wear a dress—something sexy."

She pauses at the door and turns around, the wariness fully in place again.

"I won't let anyone touch you." I hold up three fingers. "Scout's honor."

Her eyes narrow, lips twist into a smirk. "You were never a Scout." There's a derisive note of knowing in her voice that makes something slide in my belly. The urge to fuck that scorn right off her face combines with the need to punch something.

She's right. I'm no Boy Scout. Never have been. My big brothers were delivering beat-downs on Nico and I before we lost our first baby teeth. We learned the art of violence at the same time we learned our alphabet. Nico perfected the fine art of strategy—how to manipulate and win against the odds—by the time he hit puberty. He showed me the ropes, protected me. My life's been easier than his and I'm not bitter, but I'm also not going to apologize, especially not to this mouthy piece of ass. These are the cards I was dealt, the family I was born into.

But I don't allow any of this to show. Instead, I toss another wink and my lady-killer smile. "You found me out."

I reach past her to open the door again. "Do as you're told—wear the dress. I'll see that you're rewarded." To put a finer point on it, I pull a five-hundred-dollar chip from my pocket and flip it into the air. She catches it, then holds my gaze as she slowly tucks it into her cleavage.

It's all I can do not to slam the door and push her

11

against it, give her a thorough strip-search to see what else she's hiding between or around those perky breasts.

"I'll see you tomorrow, then." Her voice comes out a little breathy, telling me she's not immune to the heat of my gaze.

I clear my throat. "Tomorrow." I want to slap her ass as she sashays through the door, but I manage to find some self-restraint in time.

Tomorrow, though, she may not be so lucky.

I can't fucking wait to see her in a dress. I already know the sight of her is going to make my night.

Corey

I DIAL my cousin Sondra on my way out but she doesn't answer. She's with Nico in Chicago after a blowout fight that we all thought had ended things forever. But Tacone has a hard time taking no for an answer. I have to say— Nico Tacone may be a scary motherfucker, but he is totally in deep with Sondra.

When she left him four days ago, he flipped out. He cornered me, tried to make me tell him where she'd gone, put a guy outside my house, presumably to watch for her. Sondra thought he'd been cheating on her. But I talked to everyone close to him after Sondra left, and they all had the same story. He had a family-arranged marriage contract that he was trying to get out of and Sondra is the only woman Nico's ever been serious about.

So when I got her text yesterday with a picture of a diamond ring on her left hand, I knew they'd worked it out.

I really don't know what to think about Sondra marrying a known mobster. She's always had terrible taste in men—not that my last choice was any better.

But Nico Tacone is the real deal. He's dangerous and powerful. He made my ex disappear. Not that I'm not crying over it. Dean tried to rape my cousin.

But still. Ordinary guys don't have that kind of power.

I'm not judgy about the crime thing. As the daughter of a crooked fed, I have a very jaded sense of crime and law.

But that's why I didn't want to get involved in anything that puts me close to the seedy underbelly of the organization. And the high-stakes private games will definitely do that.

I haven't seen my dad in over ten years. When he left my mom for some skanky chick in Detroit, we all breathed a sigh of relief. Does Stefano know my dad's with the FBI? Somehow I doubt it, and if he finds out, things could get hairy fast.

I really don't know how much illegal activity goes on around here, but I'm guessing it's more peripheral. Why would they need to break laws when their casino rakes in millions a year? Still, I don't want to see any of it. I don't ever want to be in a position where they have to rely on or question my loyalty.

Dammit.

Should I have told Stefano?

And why in the hell am I thinking of him as *Stefano*

and not Mr. Tacone? He reprimanded me for calling his brother by his first name.

Oh, maybe it's all the eye-fucking he did. Or the way he kissed my fingers after catching my wrist. A shiver runs through me remembering how quickly he caught and held my wrist without any trace of exertion or anger. Rather, he seemed bemused. As if he enjoyed the opportunity to show me his superior strength and hold me captive.

It's not because I want to be on a first name basis with him.

I definitely don't.

Why would I even think that? Especially after all my concerns for Sondra?

But something about that man has me squeezing my knees together every time he winks. Which is far too often.

I drive home to my small apartment. For the first time since Sondra moved into the casino and Tacone made Dean disappear, it feels too small. Even lonely.

But I'm not looking for company. I don't need to jump into another relationship.

Of course no one's chasing me for one, either. Stefano appears to be the polar opposite of my cousin's possessive and single-minded lover, Nico. He's definitely a player.

Which means sex—just once to get him out of my system—might be on the table.

CHAPTER 2

 *tefano*

I WALK through the Bellissimo like I'm king of the castle, fucking proud of the place and what Nico's built here.

I was with Nico when he talked our father into investing 1.2 million dollars to open a casino in Vegas. It wasn't enough. Hell, the gambling license alone cost over thirty grand. But Nico was smart. He knew better than to involve any investors who weren't family. Only Tacones were allowed to kick in and hold shares of the Bellissimo. And they did. He scraped together enough to get it open and built it from there.

Nico had the architects design the massive structure so it could be added onto in sections and he went classy right from the start: Italian tile, marble statues, beautiful rooms.

The first version of the Bellissimo was small, a boutique casino. Nothing cheesy about it—ever. And so it attracted high-end customers right from the start. Especially when word got out about the private games.

Nico had a business plan and a vision, and he convinced our family to invest. Still, I don't think anyone expected it would turn out like this. Now, it's a behemoth of a building—five different wings, twenty-eight stories high. Eight restaurants serve all kinds of food and it's still the classiest joint in Vegas. And the money? It fucking overflows.

Speaking of my *stronzo* brother, I've been in the Bellissimo for thirty-six hours and haven't seen the bastard. First he was out of hand looking for his woman. Now he's gone home to fix things. We've talked on the phone and already texted a dozen times, but he's too irritable to give me any good direction.

I dial his phone and he answers with the same impatience. "What is it?"

"Nice to hear from you, too. Did you get things straightened out?"

"I'm working on it."

Of course he's not going to tell me anything. He's not exactly a let's talk about our feelings kind of guy.

"You talk to Dad?"

"On my way now. Sondra's with me."

Sondra. The woman I want to meet. "Ah yes. I had to find out her name from a lovely red haired croupier last night."

"You met Corey."

"Yes. I enticed her to cheat and she tried to slap my face."

Nico snorts. "Sounds about right."

"What about Corey?" I hear the pleasant timbre of a female voice.

"Are you in the car? Put me on speaker."

"No—fuck off."

"Sondra," I raise my voice so she might hear me. "I met your cousin last night," I tell her. "I'm in love."

Her laugh is light and sweet. Nico must have put her on speaker because I hear her voice clearly. "I'm definitely hearing the Italian in you."

"No, it's true," I insist, but she's right—even before my six-month stint in Sicily with my great uncle, I'd adopted the over-the-top aggressive courting style of my parents' country of origin.

"He already got himself slapped," Nico fills in.

"Uh oh."

"*Almost* slapped," I correct. "She tried. I didn't allow it. We came to an understanding."

"She's under my protection," Nico grumbles, but he knows I don't hurt women.

"Nothing to worry about. I told you—I'm already in love." As in, *I can't wait to get those long legs wrapped around my waist so I can pound into her hard and dirty.*

Would she like it that way?

Somehow I think she would. But she's not the type to go down without a fight, and I don't have the time or attention to spare. I'm already up to my ears in work. I can see why Nico needed help running things.

"Listen, Stefano." Nico takes the phone off speaker. He's got a serious tone to his voice.

"Yeah?"

"If things go sideways, I need you to take care of…"

I understand what he's saying—all too well. I think chances are slim he'll die, but you never know. Our father's in prison and Junior, our oldest brother, is a dick.

"I will protect what you love," I say quietly, making the vow of it ring in my voice. I know that's what he's asking; he wants to know Sondra will be safe.

"Thank you." Nico's voice is gruff.

"Good luck, Nico. Let me know how it goes."

"Yeah." He hangs up and I shake my head.

My brother's had a stupid marriage contract hanging over his head since we were kids. It was a way for our father to bind our family to another. Total stupidity, but signed in blood. Nico's just been pretending it will never happen all these years, but now he's in love. And she left him when she found out he had a fiancée.

Poor bastard. But if anyone can figure shit out when he needs to, it's Nico.

Look at what he did with this place.

It's bizarre to think of my brother in a committed relationship. I sure as hell hope he finds happiness.

Me? I don't do committed. Ever.

I'm a ladies man. I love sex, but the rest of it? A relationship?

No thanks.

Corey

I'M uneasy about working the private game tonight. I don't know if it's my spidey sense alerting me to potential trouble or if I'm being paranoid. It's the same uneasy feeling I had about Sondra dating Nico.

There's danger at the Bellissimo and until this point, I always managed to stay out of it.

Still, I'm going to be well-paid. And although this might not help me when push comes to shove, my cousin has the owner's ear. Of course, he didn't think twice about making Dean disappear.

I wear a clingy red dress—the one Sondra borrowed last week when she got herself into trouble flirting with another man to make Nico jealous.

It molds to my body, showing off my cleavage with a plunging neckline and my long legs with a provocative slit up the side.

I'm not dressing for Stefano. I'm *not.*

Okay, yeah, he might have been on my mind as I showered and dressed. I might have paid a little more attention to my makeup and hair tonight than usual.

But that's not because I hope anything will happen. Getting involved with Stefano Tacone is the last thing I'm interested in—the very last! But that doesn't mean I don't enjoy a little male attention, especially from a man who makes my body light up when he's nearby.

I park in the employee parking area and strut into the casino, my purse clutched under my arm. I put it away in an employee locker.

"What are you wearing?" Tad, one of the other croupiers asks. He's okay. Pretty into himself, but nice enough. He gives me an up and down look without much interest. I'm not sure the guy is interested in anyone other than the person he sees in the mirror.

"Don't ask," I say as I pin my nametag on the dress and slam my locker shut.

"Whoa, whoa, whoa." He catches my arm. "What's going on? Did you get transferred to another department?"

"You could say that. I'm dealing for a private game tonight."

Tad's eyebrows shoot up to his hairline. "Wow. Be careful."

I nod. Okay, I wasn't being paranoid. Even regular employees think this is a bad idea. "Thanks, I will."

I head to Stefano's office, holding my head high, sinking into my croupier persona. It's an interesting one —more dominatrix than stewardess, but I still have to be approachable and friendly, especially when gamblers are warming up.

Stefano's door stands ajar and I hear him reaming out one of the floor managers. His style is different from Nico's. His body language is casual, not nearly so deadly, but the result is the same. The manager shakes in his wingtips. Which doesn't bother me a bit, because the guy is a douche.

Stefano flicks a glance at me and holds up a finger, so I take a step back to give them privacy.

A few moments later, the manager comes out, sweat dripping from his temples.

I step in and Stefano flashes his panty-melting smile, unfolding himself from where he was perched on the edge of his desk, presumably to tower over the manager in a power play.

"*Entra, bambina.* You look great." He does the fingertip kissing gesture like I'm something delicious he's going to eat. "*Perfezionare.*" He walks right up to me and reaches for my nametag, unpinning it from my dress. His fingertips brush the bare skin of my décolletage, sending a tidal wave of heat pouring between my legs.

It's far too intimate a gesture between boss and employee. I'm overly aware of his proximity—the Henry Cavill good looks, the scent of soap and light cologne, the deft movements of his fingers so close to my breasts. The man is always so damn self-assured, which shouldn't unnerve me. I'm the same way—usually.

"No, nametag, hmm?" I step back, struggling to regain my footing.

"Nah. It detracts from the, ah, view." He lets his eyes shamelessly wander over my cleavage before tossing my nametag on his desk with the same casual grace he does everything.

I frame my breasts with my hands. "Are the girls what got me this new job?" I ask drily.

He gives me a crooked smile. "They didn't hurt." Another lingering look that makes me roll my eyes. He smirks. "The game won't start for a couple hours. Walk around the floor and be my eyes. Find me at 9:30 p.m. and I'll take you upstairs."

"Be your eyes?"

He nods like I should know exactly what he means.

21

"Check security, look for anything suspicious or off, report anything you find."

I try to hide my surprise at this new duty. I'm a croupier, not a security guard, but I don't argue. At least it's a task that my tits didn't have to qualify for. Hell, it could actually be entertaining. I have a good sense for people. I can smell a rat a mile away. You might say I got it from my dad, but I try not to claim any traits of his, good or bad. And besides, he was the biggest rat of all—maybe that's how I know.

I amble through the casino, stopping to watch the bets and tables. I enjoy looking through the lens of Stefano's eyes. What would he want me to report?

He appears at my elbow an hour later. "Tell me."

I jump at the voice so close to my ear, then curse inwardly for startling. "Tell you what I saw?" I turn to face him, unnerved by how close he's standing to me.

"Mmm hmm. Your full report." He has this way of looking at me—with appreciation and warmth, but also the promise of something I know I should avoid.

I lick my lips. "Well, I'm not sure what you want to hear about. I didn't see anything big."

"What did you see?"

"I saw a cocktail waitress keep a chip when a customer dropped it. I saw a dealer slip a five dollar chip in his pocket that wasn't a tip, I saw a couple college kids attempting to count cards and failing."

"Which dealer?" All the friendliness has left Stefano's face, like stealing from the casino—even just five dollars—is an offense punishable by death.

A shiver runs down my spine when I realize how accurate that assessment might be. And I'm supposed to throw the guy under the bus.

I blink, hesitating for a moment.

Stefano's eyes don't leave my face, the intensity of his gaze ratcheting up.

"Andrew," I murmur, because I'm not sure how to get out of this without giving a name. I probably shouldn't have said anything in the first place.

"I'll tell you what I saw." Ease has returned to his face.

"What?" I manage to say.

"I saw you rebuff six different men and attract the attention of nearly three dozen more. I saw a woman who knows how to handle herself with confidence and who pays attention." He reaches out and puts a finger under my chin. I jerk away. He smirks again. "I like making you blush."

"You don't make me blush," I snap. It's an idiotic come-back since my blushes are impossible to hide. I sense one spreading across my chest and up my neck right now.

He at least has the decency to drop it. He takes my elbow. "Time to get you upstairs, *bella*. Let's go."

If anyone else took my elbow in such a bossy, controlling way, I would punch him. But it's Stefano—a sex god in a thousand dollar suit—and his deft direction actually feels right. He's like one of those ballroom dancers who can conduct a partner anywhere and everywhere simply with subtle changes in pressure of his hand at her back. I don't pull away because I enjoy the sensation of being guided by him.

And that is just ten kinds of wrong, right there.

He takes me in the elevator to a private, key-card

access only floor and lets me into a guest suite. It's been set up for gambling. The bedroom door is closed and a horseshoe shaped table sits in the middle of the room with slim high top leather padded chairs around it. No chair for me. I take my spot behind the table and check the rolly cart holding my chips and five decks of cards still in their wrappers.

"Same rules as downstairs. Only thing different will be the minimum and upper bids, *capiche*?"

I nod at Stefano's clipped instructions.

He produces a water bottle, which he places beside me. "This is for you. Leo will be here the entire time. If any of them give you trouble, just signal him."

"Where will you be?" I don't know why I ask. It's stupid. It's not like I'm afraid without him.

Maybe I am, just a little.

"I have to run shit. With Nico gone, there are fires to put out. Don't worry, no one's going to touch you. If they do, I'll have Leo break their fingers."

Corey

Mr. Donahue. That's how the guy is introduced, and I get an *off* vibe from him right away. For one thing, he's late. I've been dealing poker for two hours with three other guys who showed up tonight and they're not pleased with letting someone new into the game.

Two of them cash out. The third—Mr. Smith—stays

but that's because he's down three hundred grand. He's probably hoping to win something off Donahue.

"Where's Nico Tacone?" Donahue demands once he's sitting and his chips are in front of him.

"Mr. Tacone isn't here tonight," I say smoothly, dealing the cards.

Donahue looks pissed. "Why not? He invited me personally. I was told I'd be playing poker with him."

My eyes narrow slightly. I doubt that's true. I flick a glance to Leo, at the door. He's not normal casino security or management. He's an import from Chicago. Part of the Family, if you know what I mean. I've worked at the Bellissimo long enough to know the insiders.

Leo's upper lip curls like he wants to shove his fist in the guy's mouth, but he just gives me a small shrug.

"I don't know who told you that, Mr. Donahue, but it won't be happening. It's your bet."

The guy looks pissed off, but he plays.

"Stefano Tacone's here," Mr. Smith grunts after he places his bet.

Donahue turns on him. "Oh yeah? Who's he? Another Tacone son?"

That should've been my clue—he referred to Nico and Stefano as *sons*, not brothers, but it doesn't register as any more strange than the rest of the man's behavior.

"Nico's brother. I met him when I came in. He'll be back," Smith sagely provides.

Donahue sniffs and settles in to play. He's a shitty player—distracted and impatient. Like Stefano last night, he doesn't fit into the normal categories of big gambler, yet he's betting thousands at a time. Is he just here to see

Nico? Is that why he was so pissed he wasn't here? Maybe he has some kind of *Family* business to take up with him and it has to be in person.

He's lost three rounds to Smith when Stefano walks in.

"Ah. Here is Mr. Tacone now," Smith says, pushing his chips across the table toward me. "I believe that must be my cue to take my winnings and go."

I count him in and return a stack of eight ten-thousand-dollar chips as Stefano saunters in, a cigar box in his hand.

"Sorry I couldn't be here for the whole game, gentlemen. I hope you enjoyed yourselves." He offers a cigar to Smith, who takes one, but doesn't stay to light it.

And that's when all hell breaks loose.

Donahue knocks his tumbler of whiskey over and it rolls to the floor. He leans over to pick it up, placing the broken glass on the table as he stands. "So you're one of the Tacone boys?" There's malice in his face, and I realize his hand has been in his pocket since he stood up. I try to signal Stefano, but he's already walking toward the man, answering him.

Stefano's signature charm is present, but he's guarded. "Yes, I'm Stefano. Do you know my family?"

Donahue pulls his hand from his pocket, holding a tiny pistol. "This is for my brother," he says, the gun wobbling in his shaking hand.

Two shots fire at the same time.

I throw the table I'm behind forward. A scream leaves my mouth.

Donahue goes down, a bullet between his eyes. Both

Stefano and Leo have guns out, arms straight in front of them.

My ears ring with the sound of the shots.

For a moment, no one moves. I'm rooted to the floor, shock plunging through me like a bolt of lightning, rooting my feet to the floor..

Stefano swears in Italian and puts his pistol in a holster under his arm. "How did he get a gun in here? Wasn't he searched for weapons?"

My body shakes—teeth chatter. I can't tear my eyes from the dead man. "I-I think he pulled it from his boot, or pant leg," I provide, remembering he had ducked under the table.

"Who is he?" Leo asks.

"No idea." Stefano stoops and removes Donahue's ID and wallet. "Get Sal and Tony up here to help you get rid of the body."

Leo lifts his chin in my direction. He still hasn't put his gun away. "What about her?"

Ice cold shoots through my veins like daggers. *What about me?* Oh God, I'm a witness. Is he asking if he should kill me, too?

Stefano examines me with an inscrutable look that seems to last a millennia. I don't breathe. "I'll take care of her."

"Yeah? You sure?"

Stefano doesn't take his gaze from me. He gives a single nod.

Leo mutters something and tucks what appear to be zip-ties in Stefano's jacket pocket.

The room swoops and spins.

I am so fucked.

~

Stefano

Vaffanculo. Why in the fuck did I let an outsider deal a private game? Bringing Corey Simonson up here was the worst mistake. Now I have a witness to murder on my hands.

Corey's smart enough to understand the position she's in. She takes a step backward, her normally shrewd blue eyes wide with shock. "W-wait. Why don't you just call the cops?" Her voice squeaks, a higher pitch than usual. "It was self-defense. I'm your witness."

"That's not how we're doing this." I keep my voice smooth, my face expressionless. I haven't figured out what in the hell I'm going to do with her yet. "Come here." I beckon to her with what I consider my take charge command.

She takes another step back, glancing around for exits. There aren't any, except the one I'm blocking.

Leo barks coded orders into his comms unit.

I don't want Corey to see any more of our men implicated in this scene.

"Corey, *now.*" I make my voice sharp and urgent.

It works. She skitters forward, around the table she so wisely upended. Amazing reflexes.

I catch her elbow and propel her out of the suite, moving swiftly toward the elevators. I don't really have a plan yet, other than to get Corey away from the scene of the crime.

When we get in, we both stand facing the doors, like we're strangers. "I don't understand why you don't call the cops." She's pulled herself together enough that her voice almost sounds normal.

"And I'm not going to explain Family business to you," I tell her curtly. Which is the only answer I have. Yeah, it was self-defense. But that *stronzo* who pulled a gun on me wasn't some wacko off the street. He had a beef with the Family—probably my father. I'm not going to open that can of worms with the local cops and trust them to sort it out with me coming out on top. No fucking way.

So it turns out Corey's not as pulled together as I thought because she suddenly lunges for the elevator control panel, smacking buttons.

I catch her wrist and wrap it around her waist, pull her back against me. "*Stop*. You're panicking."

Her body trembles against mine. "I won't tell anyone. I know it was self-defense." Her voice wobbles at the end and I curse, realizing she's crying.

And of course, the elevator has to stop at that moment and let people on.

I release her wrist and cup her nape, turning her to face me, so her face is angled away from the people who get in.

She stares straight ahead at my chest, eyes still swimming with tears. I pull a silk handkerchief from my suit pocket and slip it into her hand. That's when I notice the blood—tiny splatters stain the smooth column of her neck.

When she's finished wiping her tears, I take the hand-kerchief back and dab at the stains, using the moisture of her tears to get it off. If possible, she goes even more pale, probably realizing what I'm rubbing at.

The elevator stops on the first floor and everyone gets out, but I keep my hand at Corey's neck, not allowing her to move. I hit the button for the parking level.

I don't know what my plan is, really. Drive her home, have a talk. Make sure she knows bad shit's going to happen if she ever opens her mouth about what she saw. It's not really well-formulated yet. I'm just responding to the sense of urgency to get her away from the dead guy.

When the elevator opens at the garage level, Corey panics again. She grasps the handrail inside the elevator and hangs on, digging her heels in when I try to escort her out. I tug her waist, but she doubles over. If I'm going to get her out, it's going to take some serious manhandling.

Which under different circumstances might be appealing.

"I'm not getting in a car with you! I know what's going to happen."

"Calm down. What do you think is going to happen? I'm not going to kill you—is that what you think?"

"Just let me go!" she splutters, pitching away from me and then whirling and kneeing me hard in the nuts.

I'd like to say I kept my cool. I don't hit women—*ever*. My ma raised me better than that.

But I'm not above spanking a girl's ass. Especially when it belongs to a beautiful woman. I yank one of the zip-ties Leo put in my pocket out—which I'd had no intention of using. Wrangling her wrists together, I cinch the plastic strip around them and tighten it up.

"You need to calm the fuck down," I grit through clenched teeth. I pin her hands against the elevator wall and bring my hand down to smack her ass.

I don't hold back. My balls are throbbing and each spank satisfies the part of me she unmanned with that low blow. Of course, now my cock starts swelling, renewing the pain.

The elevator doors close and it lurches into motion. I put my keycard in the elevator and hit the floor with my suite without releasing her wrists from the wall.

Then I resume her punishment. She gasps and twists as I lay down slap after slap.

"Okay!" she cries.

"I'm sorry I kneed you in the balls, Stefano," I prompt with another slap.

"I'm sorry I kneed you in the balls, Stefano," she mutters.

I turn her and slam my lips down on hers.

She freezes for one moment, probably taken aback by my change in tactics, but then she responds. Her lips move against mine, body softens. I hold her nape with one hand, her ass with the other.

The elevator doors open.

"All right, let's try this again. You will walk out of this elevator nicely this time." I propel her through the door.

She allows it. "Where are you taking me?"

"To my room."

Her footsteps stall and I have to tug her toward my door. "Why? What are you going to do with me?"

31

The truth? I have no idea.

I key open my door and thrust her through, following and shutting the door. She immediately turns around and tries to tug the door handle back open despite the limited movement allowed by her bound wrists.

I reach around to catch the knob and she shoves her ass back. My cock goes rock hard at the contact.

"If you keep rubbing that sexy ass against me, you're going to be in a different kind of trouble."

She freezes, breath catching and holding. But when she speaks, scorn laces her words. "Are you saying you're going to rape me?"

It's meant to shut me down, but her bravado turns me on even more. I cup her throat with one hand, not squeezing tight enough to scare her, but enough to hold her head in place against my shoulder as my other hand slides down the front of her short dress. I don't hesitate—it's not in my genes. I find the skin of her thigh and trace it up under her dress to cup her mons.

"Soaking wet," I breathe against her ear, triumph punching my cock out against my pants. "Is it rape if you want it?"

"I don't want it," she lies.

I slip my fingers under the gusset of her miniscule panties and stroke along her honeyed slit. "Then I won't touch you," I lie right back to her.

She bites her lip against a moan when I dip a finger into her ready entrance. "No," she says, but it sounds more like a *yes* than anything.

"No?" My finger slides out, drags up and circles her

clit. Her hips jerk against me, and my hand closes tighter around her neck. "You want me to stop, baby?"

"Yes," she pants.

I stop moving my finger but keep it there, her clit pulsing against my digit, giving her away. But I'm not going on.

I don't force women, and she told me to stop.

Regrettably. I would love the privilege of getting Corey off.

I pull my finger away. "You tell me when you want it, baby, and I'll give it to you good." I don't release her throat.

~

Corey

MY HIPS WRITHE in a circle like I'm seeking out his hand again.

Traitorous body.

I'm so fucking confused right now, I can't think straight. A minute ago, I was sure Stefano planned to throw me over the Hoover Dam. Now I'm in a different kind of trouble, as he so eloquently put it.

It's a much preferred trouble, despite my protests.

"Come here." Stefano hooks his index finger through the zip-tie holding my wrists and tugs me further into his suite like a farmer leading his cow. It's the same style suite Sondra's been staying in here, with a kitchenette and living room area.

He doesn't bring me to the bedroom, but to the kitchen, leaving me at the table while he gets a bottle of water from the refrigerator. I lean my butt on the table because my legs are too wobbly to stand. Stefano returns and cracks open the bottle, holding it to my lips.

I lift my bound hands to take it myself and drink. "You got anything stronger?" I ask after I've downed half the bottle.

Stefano gives me that lazy grin and walks back to the kitchen, returning with a bottle of Glenlivet and two tumblers. He pours us each a couple fingers of scotch and holds one out for me. "*Saluti.*" He clinks his glass against mine.

I throw the scotch back, hoping the burn will scorch the memory of what happened upstairs right out of my mind.

"So, basically, I'm an accessory now." It hits me like a concrete block on my toes.

Stefano shrugs like accessory to murder means nothing to him. "That would never hold." He crowds into me, pushing my knees apart to stand between them. I still can't figure out if this is seduction or a scare-tactic.

"So you're not planning on killing me." He already said so, but I guess I don't believe him.

He reaches out to cup my face, his thumb brushing my cheek lightly. "*Cara,* if I was going to kill you, you'd already be dead."

I try to ignore the warmth his touch produces, the urge to nuzzle into his hand. It's just because I'm in shock and I've lost my mind. "Why let me live? Because of Sondra?"

Stefano shakes his head. "I don't want you dead." He drops his thumb to my lips and traces them. I hold still because despite his assurance, I'm still his captive. The zip-tie on my wrists prove it. "I don't kill innocents." Something flickers behind his dark eyes. "Despite what you may think about me."

I find my cheeks heating, which annoys me. "I don't think about you."

He smiles because we both know it's a lie.

I wet my lips with my tongue and he tracks the movement, hunger flaring in his chocolate brown eyes. "So what are you going to do with me?"

He tilts his head to the side. "I'm figuring that out, *bambina*."

"Th-there's something I better tell you." I don't want to bring this up—I really don't. But if he finds out another way, he may shoot first and ask questions later.

He arches a brow.

I lick my lips again. "I don't talk to my dad. Like, we're totally estranged, and that's a good thing."

Stefano's eyes narrow. I'm sure he's wondering where in the hell I'm going with this.

"But he's a fed. An FBI agent," I blurt.

Stefano curses in Italian, a long string of words I don't understand but get the meaning. He tugs my ass off the table and starts searching me in quick, pissed off movements, running his fingers along the neckline of my dress, around the insides of my bra.

If I weren't more than a little afraid of Stefano Tacone in warrior mode, I might remark at the similarity of my situation with Sondra's. This was how she met Nico, after all. He strip-searched her for a wire when he found her cleaning his bathroom.

Stefano drags his large palms up my thighs, around to the back, sliding a finger over the G-string through my crack. He checks the gusset of my panties, sparing me any comments about how wet I am this time.

And yeah—my panties are damp again. I shouldn't be turned on by Stefano's rough and thorough search, but I am. He lifts my dress up to my waist, hikes it up to my armpits before he realizes it's not coming off. Not unless he removes the zip-tie.

He pulls me across the kitchen, where he grabs a pair of scissors from the drawer.

I think he's going to cut off the zip-tie, but instead the fucker slices through the fabric of my dress.

I shove at him, even though it's too late. "Jesus! You don't have to cut it, asshole. This is my favorite dress." The dress falls in shreds at my feet. I'm standing there in a black lace bra and matching G-string, a pair of black thigh-highs and my stilettos. It's quite an outfit, but he's apparently unaffected.

He yanks my bra cups down, searching visually as he runs his thumbs inside them for a second time. "Watch your mouth, I'm still your boss. I'll buy you another fucking dress if you're clean."

"I'm clean, dammit. Where else would I hide a wire? Why didn't you just cut off the zip-tie?"

He catches my jaw with grim determination. At first I think he's going to punish me for getting too mouthy, but he presses it open. "Maybe I like having you at my mercy." He flicks his brows and I register the return of his jaunty arrogance, a fraction of humor and enjoyment. Maybe that's what pisses me off. When he sweeps a finger inside to check my teeth, I bite down, hard.

"*Merda!*" He yanks his finger back and my teeth scrape over flesh. I pop them open at the taste of blood, instantly realizing I went way too far.

I tense, frozen like a rabbit, but Stefano doesn't move, other than to shake out his hand. His eyes lock on mine, blazing, but not with anger. No, with dark promise. Excitement. Like he's *glad* I bit him.

A shiver races up my spine.

"I think you must want another spanking." His voice holds deadly calm.

I can't seem to move. Can't breathe.

I fear he's right.

In a flash, he whirls me around and pushes my torso over the table. He doesn't start spanking hard like he did in the elevator, though. He just runs his hand over my bare ass cheeks and whistles.

"*Bambina*, if I knew you were hiding *this* under your dress, I would've lifted your skirt for your last punishment." He circles my ass again.

Anticipation races over my skin, flutters in my belly.

"You're still wearing my handprints." There's a rumble of appreciation in his voice, almost a purr. "Are you sore?"

"Yes," I say, infusing petulance into my words. I *am* still sore. In fact, now that he mentions it, my butt is hot and tingling. Of course, redheads register pain more than most people.

He rubs my ass. "Spread your legs, baby." His voice is no more than a murmur.

I attempt to ignore the direction, like I didn't hear it, but he kicks my feet apart. To my utter humiliation, he starts spanking my pussy. Short, deliberate taps right over my clit. My inner thigh muscles jump and shiver as he puts a little more wrist into it.

"Stefano," I gasp.

"That's right, *amore*. Say my name."

My pussy clenches, more shivers run down my legs. He smacks one ass cheek, hard.

"Ouch!"

"Mmm hmm." He slaps the other cheek, then picks up his pace, alternating one cheek then the other. The man doesn't know the definition of a light slap. Every time his palm connects with my flesh it sends shockwaves of sensation jolting through me. Pain mingled with pleasure. It's too much, and yet I don't want him to stop. I'm tragically enamored with my situation. He increases the intensity and speed another notch and I cry out. "Ouch! Hey!"

Yeah, now I want him to stop.

Definitely.

"You might remember the words I need to hear, *bella*."

"I'm sorry! I'm sorry I bit your finger, Stefano."

He stops and spins me around. "Good girl. Quick learner." Like before, he ends the punishment with a kiss. His lips crash down on mine and he bends me backward on the table, following me down. I have no choice but to wrap my legs around his waist and cradle his hips against mine. His cock presses hard and insistent against my panties, but he doesn't rush. He kisses down my neck, yanks my bra down to scrape his teeth across my nipple.

I arch into him, grind my mons against the hard bulge

in his pants. He draws my nipple into his mouth, sucks it until I feel the answering tug between my legs.

His movements are sure and confident, like he knows his way around a woman's body, yet there's also a crazy urgency, a passion behind every movement that carries me away. I can't help but respond to his touch, like he's the musician and my body's the instrument. The music he makes with me intoxicates us both.

He moves to the neglected nipple, sucking, biting, blowing air across it. Hot hands slide up my thighs. I think he's going to fuck me now. This time I'm not going to refuse.

But after he yanks my G-string down, he brings his face down to my pussy and licks into me. I cry out, my hips jacking up off the table. He holds them down and licks again, a long lick, from anus to clit.

Jesus. I didn't know that would feel so good. I've never had attention paid to my anus—never wanted attention paid there, but Stefano's unafraid.

He delves his tongue into my pussy, penetrating me, then shifts to suck my clit. He dips two fingers into me and curls them inside, rubbing my inner wall.

I tear at his hair, my juices flowing so freely I'm afraid they'll leak out of me. This is all too much and yet my body sings, glories in his touch. His thumb slides in my entrance and another finger, wet from my pussy, pushes at my anus.

Once again, my hips fly off the table. He holds me down, re-affixing his lips to my clit, sucking the nubbin hard. He penetrates my asshole with a finger.

I'm mortified.

Exhilarated.

The sensations flow through me too quickly to process. My body belongs to him. I have no choice but to surrender, to let go and let him play me, his instrument. And he does.

Within moments, I'm orgasming—*hard*. When I scream, he covers my mouth with his hand, still pumping his fingers in and out of me. It's miraculous and horrible. I'm undone.

And when it's over, vulnerability and a pinch of shame rush in like an ocean tide. I choke back a sob against his palm.

～

Stefano

O*H FUCK.*

I release my hand from Corey's mouth to see her face. She turns away from me, shoving her knuckles between her teeth. She's crying. Or trying not to.

Fuck, fuck, fuck. I was so sure she wanted it. Her body responded like I was its master. She never said no, never pushed me away.

My cockstand drops to nothing. I don't get off on rape. At all.

I quickly pull her up to sit, tugging her panties back into place. "*Cazzo*, Corey." I search her face, trying to decipher the tears. Was it just too much? Sometimes chicks cry after orgasm, especially a big one. Or did she feel forced?

I fucking hope not.

"Are you—" I don't even know what I'm going to say, but she thumps me on my chest with her bound hands.

"Stop looking at me, Stefano."

Relief washes over me. She's okay. I can tell by the familiarity she uses—calling me by name, smacking my lapel. She wouldn't do that if she were truly scared, truly felt forced. She's raw from the orgasm and the fucked up situation, that's all.

I cup the back of her neck with my clean hand and pull her against me. She hits my chest with her forehead and stays there, gulping and sniffing. I stroke my thumb along the tendrils of hair at her nape until her breath slows. Then I release her. "Sit tight," I warn, pointing a bossy finger at her. "Don't move or I'll spank your ass again."

She scowls at me, which I take as a good sign. She still has spirit. I have no interest in breaking her.

When I come back, she's pulled herself together. "Stefano," she says, holding her bound wrists out to me. "Let me go. I'm not going to talk, I promise. My cousin, who's like a sister to me, is marrying your brother. I'm practically part of the family now."

My eyebrows shoot up, because Nico—the *stronzo*—hasn't told me he's marrying the girl yet. I hope that means the shit with the Family is done. "That true? They getting married?"

She bobs her head. "She texted me a picture of the ring."

I don't know why, but that makes me insanely happy

41

for the guy. Nico is one seriously intense motherfucker. He's never attempted to make himself happy, maybe because the marriage contract with Guisseppe Pachino's daughter's been hanging over his head all these years.

I crowd into her space again. It's hard to take her seriously when she looks like she stepped off the pages of a classy men's magazine. The thigh-highs and heels are pretty much blowing my mind. "What does that make us, then?" I unhook her bra in the back and slide the straps down, even though I know they'll catch on her zip-tied wrists.

"There is no *us*," she snaps, but doesn't resist my touch. "Stefano, let me go. Please."

I put a finger under her chin. "I can't," I tell her. *Won't.* "Not yet."

Her breath quickens, which makes her pink-tipped breasts bob with each inhale. "Why not? What are you going to do with me?"

"I haven't decided yet."

"Please." Her voice rises. "You can call Nico—Mr. Tacone…" she trails off, though, uncertainty flickering over her face. Which doesn't surprise me. I can count the number of people who are certain of what Nico will do or say on one hand.

"I will certainly talk to Nico," I say smoothly. "In the meantime, you're staying here." I tug the bra tangled around her wrists.

"Are you going to cut that off, too?" she snaps.

"Yes, I think I will." I pick up the scissors. It's not to be a dick, but because the idea of buying her new bras gets me harder than a rock. I'm going to enjoy having Corey Simonson at my mercy.

Very much.

She huffs as I snip the bra straps and free the fabric from her wrists.

"Come, *bella*." I take her tangled fingers and lead her toward the bedroom.

She balks, digging her heels in and pulling against me.

"Relax. I'm putting you to bed *to sleep*. It's late and I need to get my ass back out on the floor."

She shakes her head. "Stefano, please. This is fucked up. Just let me go. I don't understand why I'm your prisoner."

"I need to be sure of you, *bella*. So for now, you stay." I nudge her toward the bathroom. "There's the restroom. Use it if you need to, because you won't have a chance while I'm gone."

Panic flares in her eyes, but she tosses her long red hair on her way to the toilet. While she's gone, I yank the casino phone out from the wall and stow it in the closet. Using more zip-ties from my pocket, I make a chain with them, affixing the top one to the solid metal of the bed frame. When she returns, I pat the bed, hiding the zip-ties. She eyes me warily but approaches and tucks herself under the covers, presumably to hide her state of undress.

I catch her wrists and attach the zip-tie chain to hers.

"Hey! What the fuck?" she tugs at them.

"*Stop.*" I make my voice sharp. "Take it easy, *bella* or this zip-tie will cut into your wrists."

She glares up at me. "Oh, and you care because why?"

Because I don't want to feel bad about the way I'm treating her. And I definitely should. She doesn't deserve to be tied up to my bed. She's done nothing wrong. But I'm thinking with my dick now, and there's no way I'm letting her go. Not when I have her in such a delicious position.

I lift her bound fingers to my lips and kiss them softly. "I don't want to see red marks here." I trace my finger beneath the zip-tie, testing for tightness. "If I come back and you've worked your skin raw, I'm going to punish you again. *Capiche?*"

Her eyes fly wide, genuine fear flooding them.

"No," I say, guessing at her panicked thoughts. "I'm not a psychopath. Although I'd love to play sex games with you chained to my bed all fucking week. Be good"— I tap her nose—"or it can be arranged." I head for the door.

"Stefano!" she screams my name through clenched teeth. It's a good sign. I like her mad. I don't want her terrified.

I turn and arch a brow. "Need anything? No?" I don't give her a chance to answer. "I'll get you a toothbrush while I'm downstairs. I'll be back by dawn. Try to get some sleep."

Corey

I'M ready to murder Stefano Tacone myself. I can't figure out his game. Is he really worried about me talking? Or is he a crazy sex predator who saw an opportunity to take me captive and did so?

But no. If he was into sex crimes, he would've raped me on his kitchen table. And he didn't. He didn't even try to have sex with me. All he did was offer me pleasure.

He's definitely attracted to me; he's made that plain. But I really don't think he's going to force himself on me tonight.

With that thought, my confidence in making it through this situation takes an upturn. I witnessed a mafia murder, but I'm still alive. The man who captured me has not been cruel. In fact, other than keeping me captive, he was fairly attentive—offering me water, suggesting I use the bathroom. Blowing my mind with the orgasm of the century.

Oh fuck, what am I saying? Do I seriously already have Stockholm Syndrome? Am I bonding with my captor?

Then it hits me with a flash of cold. *Is that his intent?* How he's going to be sure of me? Get me to bond to him so I won't talk?

No, that's ridiculous. A man like Stefano Tacone does not rely on *wooing* women into silence. That's scoffable. He uses his fists. His gun.

And since he's used neither on me, I can probably assume I'm fairly safe.

I lean over the side of the bed to investigate where he attached the zip-tie. If it's to the leg of the bed, maybe I can lift it off.

No dice.

It's right to the metal frame beneath the mattress. Stefano's good. I shudder to think he's done this before.

My maneuvering twists the zip-tie around my wrists and I check my skin for marks. Yep, totally left some.

And that thought should *not* excite me.

But I could really get off on Stefano Tacone's punishments. What am I saying? I already have.

So yeah, tempting him into another one feels like a delicious danger I'd love to play with.

But despite my certainty I'd never sleep, I drift off.

I dream of mafia meetings: dangerous men with guns and tempers. My dad is there. He's the leader and he catches me spying on them. He holds me up by the hair and slaps my face like he used to when he was drinking.

I startle awake, sweating.

"Shh, *bambina.* You're safe here." Stefano Tacone appears in my dream, brushing my hair back from my face.

No.

Stefano Tacone is in the bed.

I blink my eyes open. The early light of dawn spills through the curtains.

"Go back to sleep, *bella.* It's too early to be awake."

I try to turn toward his voice, but plastic bites into my wrists and I whimper.

"Okay, okay. I'll free you." The mattress pitches and he climbs off. When he appears in my line of vision, he's holding a deadly hunter's knife. He crouches in front of me and slices the zip-tie holding my wrists. His stubble has grown overnight and weariness tugs down the corners of his eyes. "You stay in this bed, though," he warns.

I rub the chafed skin, rolling over to face the middle of

the bed where he lies down. He takes one of my wrists and strokes the marks with his thumb.

"Naughty, babe," he murmurs, closing his large hand around my wrist as his eyelids close.

I stare at his handsome face in the dark, listen as his breath slows. He smells like the casino—like scotch and money and old leather. I consider trying to slip out of his grasp, but I can't seem to find the motivation. I might have to admit to myself that I enjoy being his captive. Leaving now would be a disappointment. Eventually, my inhales match his and I slide back into a dream. Only this time, I'm tied to Stefano's bed.

CHAPTER 3

 *tefano*

Oh, no you don't.

My hand closes around Corey's wrist. She's trying to sneak away from me.

Her electric blue eyes meet mine. They hold no trace of fear or remorse, which makes me want to kiss her senseless. I love her confidence. Her verve. I have her half-naked in my bed and she's not unnerved in the least.

"I have to pee," she says. "Did you get me that tooth-brush?" Adorable. She treats this like a fucking slumber party.

"On the counter," I mumble, still coming awake. I release her wrist. She tugs the sheet off the bed to cover herself as she pads to the bathroom.

"Leave the door cracked open, *amore*. I need to hear what you're doing."

"Fuck you, Tacone," she calls back.

"Still your boss," I remind her.

Even though she's mouthy, she does as she's told.

Smart woman.

When she comes back, she walks straight to the dresser and pulls out a drawer.

They're all empty. I don't plan in staying in this guest suite, but I haven't bothered to kick Sal out of my suite on the top floor yet. He moved in there when I left for Sicily six months ago.

"You looking for something to wear?"

"Yeah," she says, turning to face me. "Where are your clothes?"

"Come back to bed. You'll get clothes when you earn them. Right now you have a punishment coming."

She has the nerve to roll her eyes and I have to suppress a grin.

"Now, *bambina*."

She examines one wrist. "How do you know you didn't do this putting them on?"

I shrug. "I know. Besides, you're getting punished no matter what." I cup my aching balls through my boxer briefs. "If my balls are still bruised, *bambina*, your ass is going to be raw. That's just casino rules. *Capiche*?"

She winces, glancing at my cock, which surges to attention. "Sorry?"

I climb off the bed. "You will be. Come here, *bella*." She darts for the door and my dick grows hard because I get to lunge for her, pick her up and carry her to the bed.

I toss her down in the center of it and yank the sheet away.

She doesn't appear particularly frightened or pissed off, which bodes well for me finally getting my cock into her. Climbing into bed last night and not claiming her was an exquisite torture. I didn't sleep enough to dream, but if I had, I'm sure it would've been all about those pouty lips stretched around my length, those bright blue eyes gazing up at me.

"Let's see... what to do to my beautiful prisoner." I stare down at her, drinking in the sight of her lovely breasts, the way her red hair spreads out on the mattress like flames. Somehow her delectable stockings stayed on all night long. Her cheeks are flushed, eyes dilated. I know she wants this, even if she won't admit it.

I reach to her thighs and grab one stocking in each hand to yank them down.

She kicks. "Jesus! You have to ruin those too?"

I roll her over and slap her ass, then twist her wrists behind her back and use one of the stockings to tie them together. "Too mouthy, *bella*. I like your spunk, but I require a little more respect."

"I'm sorry, Stefano."

A chuckle barrels out from me before I can stop it. "You do learn fast, don't you, *amore*?" I tug her hips up to bring her knees under her so she's on an angle with her face on the bed and her ass in the air. "Mmm, now that's pretty."

The fact that she holds still tells me she's all in. I slap her ass a couple times with my hand, then retrieve my belt from the closet. I use the last six inches of it to lightly slap her, warming her cheeks and backs of her thighs with gentle licks. Then I let out a little more length and slap it hard across the center of her ass.

She yelps and lists to the side. "Ow!"

"Two more just like that and we can get to your reward. Now hold your position. You don't want this belt hitting you somewhere that doesn't feel good."

"Who says it feels good at all?"

I give a dark chuckle. "Feels good to me." I whip her again, laying a neat stripe just below the first one. She gasps, but holds still. "Good girl." I swing a third time, then toss the belt onto the bed beside her. "Now for your reward."

I untie her wrists and roll her over. Her eyes are glassy, lips parted. "Do you want a reward, Corey?"

She nods, eyes locked on mine as I climb up onto my knees on the bed and slide my hands under her hips to cup her ass. She bends her knees up to accommodate me.

I lower my face to her cunt and nip her through the scrap of panties. "You have to say it out loud. I don't want any misunderstandings."

"I want my reward," she says quickly.

I laugh and nip her again. "Tell me what you want me to do, *amore*. Be very clear."

She swallows.

I know she's full of bluster, but I'm actually not sure whether Corey Simonson knows how to ask for what she wants.

Turns out she does.

"I want your mouth on me—like last night. And…"

I pull her panties to one side and drag my tongue up her slit. "And?" I arch a brow.

"I-I want you to fuck me."

Victory dance.

I knew we'd get here sooner or later, but I'm fucking thrilled she made it so easy.

I pull her panties off. They're the only piece of clothing I haven't ruined. I might need to remedy that. But I don't have time to think about clothing when her pussy's wet and waiting.

I cup her hot ass in my hands and lick into her. She tries to arch off the bed, but I shift my hands to pin her pelvis down, hold her still for the onslaught of my tongue. I trace her inner lips, penetrate her with my thumb. I flick and tease her clit until it's swollen and the hood pulls back.

"Play with your breasts," I order.

"Wha—" She lifts her head, looking beautifully befuddled. A surge of manly pride shoots through me. *I did that to her.*

"Pinch those nipples. Make them hard." I wait until she complies before I return to pleasuring her. She arches her lower back from the bed, rocking her pelvis toward my face. I go slowly, dipping two fingers into her and arcing them to stroke her inner wall.

She gasps and clenches around my fingers, inner thighs clamping down on my shoulders.

"Stefano."

"That's it, baby. Say my name."

"I need it," she says.

Oh, fuck me. *I need to give it to you so hard, baby.* But I

53

also don't want this to end. I enjoy having Corey trembling and gasping my name like I'm the only man in the universe who can give her what she needs.

I ease my fingers out of her and pick up one of her stockings. She watches me climb over her with heavy-lidded eyes, but they fly wide when I catch her wrists and quickly tie them together.

"You have a bondage thing, Stefano?" Her voice is soft and breathy, no trace of the harsh judgment she usually infuses.

"Only with you, *bambina*." It's mostly true. Sure, I've tied girls up before, smacked their asses, bossed them around. But with Corey it's far more interesting. She's not submissive by nature, so taking her power away gives her a far greater release. And frankly, I *want* to conquer her this way.

I hold her wrists down and work one of her nipples with my teeth and tongue. She writhes beneath me. *"Stefano."* She pops her pelvis up to hit my aching cock. She needs it bad.

So do I.

"Beg for it." It's a challenge. I know it will piss her off and it does. She rolls her eyes.

"You want to hear you're good?"

I cup her mons and stroke my middle finger slowly along her juicy slit.

"You're fucking good. So damn good." She rolls her head around on the bed with a wanton moan.

"Beg."

"You're also a cocky—"

I release her nipple with a pop and arch a warning brow.

"—arrogant, controlling bastard who's keeping me prisoner."

I remove all touch, backing up and pulling her wrists toward the headboard where I wind an end of the stocking around the post. "Badly played, *amore.*"

She pants, watching me with those bright blue eyes. Her legs swish restlessly on the bed.

I walk to the closet and rummage in my suitcase for the vibrator. Yes, I travel with it. You never know when you might need to pleasure a woman. I twist it to turn it on and saunter back to my lovely captive.

"Open your thighs, *bella.*"

She tugs at her bound wrists, eyes on the vibrator, legs still dancing.

I climb over her. "Don't make me ask twice," I murmur.

Her knees fall open the moment the vibe hits her clit. I stroke it slowly up and down her slit, feed it into her, then remove it and tease her clit. I continue this pattern until her pants become whines, her head rolls around with impatience.

Finally, I insert the vibrator into her and leave it, then I walk away.

"Hey!" she cries indignantly as I head to the bathroom.

I ignore her and wash my hands and face, brush my teeth.

"Stefano Tacone, you bastard. Get back here. *Please.*"

"Baby, I'm not going to warn you again—don't call me names." I come out of the bathroom, drying my hands.

It's not really that I give a shit. But I have a reputation. I can't have her disrespecting me in front of anyone else.

"I'm sorry." She seeks my gaze with pleading one. "Please don't do this. Please."

"What do you need? Ask me sweetly."

She grimaces, but lifts her chin. "I want your big Italian cock, okay? Are you going to give it to me?"

I can't help but laugh. I pull the vibrator out of her and toss it on the bed. "I like you, Corey Simonson." I slip my hand in my boxer briefs and pull out my cock. "Very much." I snap open a condom and roll it on.

"I wish I could say the same, but you know—" She looks up at her tied wrists.

~

Corey

"Oʜ, you'll like it, *bella*. I'll make sure of it." Stefano rubs the head of his sheathed cock over my swollen opening.

I moan, and my eyeballs roll back in my head. So help me God, I know he will. I'm freaking *dying* for Stefano to get me off. My whole body's fevered and needy for him. And I have no doubt he'll deliver everything I need.

I bend my knees up in offering.

The truth is, I'm enjoying my imprisonment with Stefano Tacone way too much. The man is far too sexy for his own good. For my own good.

He eases in, this thick member stretching me wide.

Once seated, he withdraws, grips the tops of my thighs and plows back in, bumping my ass with his balls.

It's exactly what my body craves.

Stefano lets out a growl of pleasure, holding me tighter as he increases his speed. "Yes," I whisper, closing my eyes.

"Look at me, *bambina*."

I don't know why he wants me to look, but I crack my lids and stare up at him as he thoroughly fucks me. It's more intense with our gazes locked—way more intense. Stefano's lids droop, but a muscle in his jaw ticks as he shoves in with powerful thrusts. His eyes blaze with dark heat, animalistic desire.

I find myself wishing he'd taken off his t-shirt so I could watch those bulging muscles on his arms and chest flex in naked glory. Fuck it; he made me ask for sex. I can ask for this, too.

"Take off your shirt, Stefano." I don't even ask.

His eyes flare and a slow smile spreads over his face as he continues to pump in and out of me. He drags his t-shirt off and tosses onto the floor. "Better?"

My mouth waters, and I'm suddenly dying to drag my tongue over all that hard flesh. His chiseled chest is covered in dark curls with a happy trail that leads to his cock. Washboard abs. Ripped shoulders. No tattoos. That surprises me.

He drops to rest on his hands beside my ribs, bringing his face close to mine. "Like what you see?"

I pop my hips to meet his thrusts, take him deeper. "Yeah."

He twists his lips over mine in one demanding kiss,

then pushes back up to his knees and rolls mine up to my shoulders.

I gasp at the new angle, the intensity of sensation. And that's when he picks up the vibrator. He turns it on and pushes the tip up against my clit.

"No!" I wriggle, pre-orgasmic alarm flashing through me.

"Fucking give it to me," he snarls.

I'm not even sure what he means, but he's relentless with the vibrator and his teeth-rattling thrusts. I explode. Shatter. Disintegrate. I'm nothing but bucking hips and screams while he wrenches the orgasm from me the same forceful way he demands everything.

My inner muscles clench around his cock, squeezing.

I realize he's making one long continuous growling sound. His nostrils flare and he bares his teeth. The sound peaks into a roar and he thrusts deep, ass bucking and jerking as he comes.

I come some more, another flutter of muscles clenching around his cock, milking it.

He drops down onto me and bites my shoulder, still rocking into me, but sweetly now. My body revels in every area of contact, post-coital pleasure spreading through me like an inkblot, making the whole fucked up night seem like nothing more than a prelude to this.

And that's just the sex talking. Pay no attention to this cock-inspired bliss. I am still a prisoner here. And he's still my keeper.

Even if he does know how to make my body sing.

He eventually pulls out and tosses his condom in the

trashcan by the bed, then lies beside me, stroking his hand up my belly.

I have a huge birthmark, an ugly splotch of red that stretches across my side, and I grow suddenly self-conscious when he starts tracing it with his finger.

"Don't."

"What? It's beautiful. You're beautiful. How do you not have a boyfriend?"

I wrinkle my nose. "What makes you think I don't?"

His sexy lips quirk. "I figured you would've said something the first time I kissed you."

"Fair enough," I concede.

"I don't get it—woman like you. How do you not have a whole legion of men around you who fall on their knees to worship you forever? I would think one taste and they'd be lost."

Something twists in my middle, the sick feeling of betrayal and failure. "Yeah, well, my last boyfriend turned out to be a snake. And your brother made him disappear."

Stefano arches a brow. "Permanently?"

A shiver runs up my spine at the confirmation of what could've been.

"No, I don't think so."

"What happened?"

Anger shoves up in my chest, hot and searing. "Apparently *one taste of me,* as you suggested, was not enough, and he thought it would be cool to force-fuck my cousin, too. He didn't manage because Nico showed up."

Stefano mutters something and rubs a hand across his mouth. "How is he not dead?"

Right. That was my assessment of what Nico's capable

of, too. "Sondra was there, screaming for him to stop. So he did. Told him to leave the state or he'd kill him."

Stefano stares down at me. I think he's going to tell me what an idiot Dean was, or how I'm better off, but he surprises me. "You're still pissed," he observes.

I frown because, *yeah*, of course I'm pissed. But I also realize what it means. I'm not over Dean. And I really want to be.

"You didn't get to knee him in the nuts before he left."

I'm surprised by the laugh that tumbles from my lips. "Yeah, that might've helped."

"I could find him for you and haul him back," Stefano offers. "Let you turn his balls blue like you turned mine."

I laugh again.

"I'm serious. I would do that for you in a heartbeat."

His brown eyes are warm now, flicks of gold and green glittering in the sunlight that filters through the curtains.

"Is that your version of a knight in shining armor?"

"Yeah. I guess." He rolls away, off the bed and heads to the bathroom. I hear the shower turn on.

Did I offend him? Was that a slight against the type of man he is? A mobster?

No. That's impossible. Stefano Tacone is all confidence and swagger. Why would he care what I think?

Except I can't push away the nagging idea I somehow hurt him. Which for some reason kills the post-orgasm buzz I was floating on.

 *tefano*

I ORDER ROOM service for breakfast and call down to the front desk to have work out clothes delivered in her size. It's one of the perks offered at the Bellissimo. I also call the clothing shop in the casino and ask for a fashion consultant to pick out a variety of red dresses to replace the one I cut and other clothing and to deliver them to the room.

Then I get with Al Sampson, the detective who does background checks on people for the casino and ask for everything on Corey Simonson.

"I already have a partial file on her," he tells me, "from when I ran her cousin, Sondra Simonson. I'll send over what I have and keep digging."

"You sending it electronically?"

"Yeah, you'll have it in two minutes."

"Thanks, Al. Appreciate it." I pocket my phone and straighten my tie.

I've ignored the naked redhead tied to my bed since my shower, which is pissing her off. I'll untie her when the food gets here, but for now she can stew.

I don't know why I'm pissed at her calling out the things that make me a Family man. It's like I'm that kid in Catholic school again. The one the others are afraid of. The one they whisper about when I'm not there and go dead silent when I ask what's up.

I never wanted to be that kid. I didn't get into fist fights—not unless really provoked. As the youngest of five Tacone boys, proving myself was never necessary. And really, it's not my style. I was more of the class clown. The smart aleck who got sent to the principal's with a smirk on his face. I generally *like* people.

And Corey's like Tosha Davis. The one I wanted to entertain but was never good enough for.

Because her dad was a politician and mine—a mobster.

So now I have the daughter of a fed tied to my bed. One who saw me kill a man last night. It's not something I'm proud of, but I had no choice. And I want her to see me as something beyond a well-suited mafia man.

Which is stupid.

I shouldn't give a shit what she thinks anyway, and I'm not entering a relationship with her.

I mean, why would I even think this way?

Except I'm not willing to untie her and let her walk out of my room, either. And if I were totally honest, I'd have to admit only a small part of my reasoning for that has to do with her watching me pull that trigger last night.

I'm usually done with a woman the moment I come. I mean, I don't mind giving her a little cuddle afterward, but I definitely don't want to hang around and eat breakfast with her.

So why am I still in this suite? It's not like I don't have a shit ton to do out in the Bellissimo.

Jesus, it's like Nico's sudden attachment to a woman has me suddenly starting one, too.

Maybe it's catching. Heh. Maybe it's some biological attraction. Like the Simonson genes match well with the Tacones'.

Okay, I'm off my fucking rocker now.

"Room service." A tap sounds at the front door. I point in warning at Corey. "Not a word, *amore*." I shut the door to the bedroom to block any view of her.

Once the server is gone, I set her free and give her one of my t-shirts to wear. "I'm having workout clothes sent up and we'll work on replacing that dress this afternoon. Come on, I ordered us some food."

I actually hadn't planned on staying to eat with her, but it's like there's this magnetic pull, keeping me here in the suite with her.

She's unusually quiet as she eats.

"You okay?" I find myself asking as I sip my coffee and observe her.

She raises her brows. "Hmm, am I okay? I got some guy's blood splattered on me last night, witnessed a murder and now am some kind of prisoner to my boss, who happens to be the guy who pulled the trigger and is also into kinky games. I don't even know what *okay* is in this situation."

It's my fucking fault for asking. What did I think she would say? But her assessment—accurate though it may be—puts my hackles up. And rather than be an asshole, I decide it's time to leave.

"I gotta work. You'll stay here. I'm keeping you close until I figure out what to do with you."

She shoots to her feet. "What's to figure out?" She spreads her hands. "I promise I won't say a word."

"Thank you. I appreciate your word for it." I say as I walk to the bedroom and grab the phone out of the drawer where I stashed it. "As soon as I'm sure of it, I'll let you go."

She looks at the phone in my hand, wariness clouding her features. "Are you going to tie me up again?"

I arch a brow. "Do I need to?"

"Uh, no. Nope. Huh uh."

I'm pretty sure she thinks she's going to walk right out of here as soon as I leave. What she doesn't know is that I put a security guy on the door. She won't be going anywhere. Not unless I want her to.

"Good. Watch some TV. Relax. I'll be back to check on you."

She sucks on her lower lip as she watches me leave. I throw a wink from the door, but I'm not feeling as jaunty as it probably looks.

In fact, I'm uneasy about the whole thing. About leaving Corey prisoner. And also about letting her go. And I don't know what the hell's wrong with me, but I think I'm actually concerned about her state of mind—her happiness.

No, it's more than that.

I'm fucking worried she'll never forgive me for this.

And that is downright unlike me.

~

Corey

FIRST THING I do after Stefano leaves is get in the shower and turn the water on hot. I need time to think.

Do I just leave? Is he testing me here? It seems like a mafia thing to test people. He's deciding if I'm trustworthy based on whether I follow his directions and stay put?

On the other hand, I'm his fucking prisoner! And if I have a chance to get away I should, right?

Only what then? I'm not going to the cops. I meant what I told him. I would never in a million years get on a witness stand against a Tacone. That's suicide. I don't care if there is a witness relocation program. Besides, Sondra's marrying his brother. These guys really are about to become family by marriage. I'm not going to snitch on my family.

And yeah, Sondra's boyfriend would be more *family* to me than my own dad. Easily.

So yeah, let's say I bolt. Then what? I want to keep my job here. I have no desire to go to the cops. I also have no desire to have Stefano Tacone put me on his wanted list.

Sort of seems like I stay put. Besides my lack of free-dom, I'm not suffering here. I've been fed. He said he's sending clothing. I've had my sexual needs tended in a blow-my-mind kinda way.

I shampoo and condition my hair. Unfortunately, there's no razor. I'm sure if I asked him for one, he'd bring it.

Which is sort of fun.

When I get over being freaked out about what's happening, it's actually quite fun. Thrilling, even.

I turn off the water and grab a towel.

A tap sounds at the door.

Shit. Must be the clothes. I wrap the towel under my armpits and open the front door a crack.

"Oh, sorry, ma'am." A security guard turns red in the face as he thrusts a Bellissimo bag toward me. "They brought this for you." He averts his gaze, staring past my shoulder instead of looking at me.

"Are you guarding this door?" I demand, suddenly outraged. I spent all that time deciding not to leave and it turns out I had no choice, anyway.

Fucking Tacone.

The guard turns even redder. "Mr. Tacone's orders, ma'am. I'm sorry." He drops the bag inside the suite and pulls the door shut in my face.

Harumph.

I pick up the bag and rummage through it. It's a tank top and yoga pants. No panties. It will have to do. I get dressed and make the bed, for lack of anything better to do. And because I'm one of those neat freaks who prefers things to be in their place.

Then I set back and do as Stefano suggested—watch TV. What the hell, there's nothing better to do.

At 1:00 p.m., room service arrives with a variety of lunch options. At 3:00 p.m., Stefano finally returns.

I bite back the "it took you long enough" in favor of something more amicable. "How are things out there?"

"Fine." He looks around the room as if for clues for what I've been up to. "What do you need here? Anything?"

Oh shit. He's just stopping in. Ready to head back out any minute. I don't want to stay cooped up here all day alone.

I clear my throat. "I, uh, could use some exercise. You know—I'm in the outfit, but nowhere to work out."

Stefano frowns and glances toward the door. Then he shakes his head.

"What?"

"Fine." A note of annoyance clips the word. "I'll take you to the fitness center." He stalks to the bedroom. When he returns, he's changed from his thousand-dollar gunmetal gray pinstriped suit into a soft hunter green t-shirt and black workout shorts. The worn t-shirt stretches around the muscles of his chest.

I resist the urge to paw the air.

"Come on, princess. I don't have all day."

I walk to the door. "Is it princess now? Funny, I'm not feeling much like a princess."

He pops my ass. "Stop sulking. Walk."

I flip him the bird over my shoulder, pushing my luck.

I push open the door and the guard steps out of the way, nodding to Stefano.

67

"Take a break. I'll message you on the comms when I need you again."

"Yes, sir. Thank you, Mr. Tacone."

Stefano answers his phone, responding to some casino business with short, decisive answers, then switches to a comms device, giving more orders as we step toward the elevator. He reaches past me and hits the elevator button for up instead of down.

"Where are we going?" I ask. The fitness center is on the tenth floor, below us.

"Private gym." Stefano flashes me a model-worthy grin and holds an arm out to usher me into the elevator.

"Oh. I didn't know there was a private gym here."

"There are lots of things you don't know about the Bellissimo," he says, circling an arm behind my back like we're on a date.

We get off on the 18th floor and Stefano leads me to a small but beautifully appointed, air-conditioned gym. Mirrors cover every wall and the floor is springy gym mat material. The smell of eucalyptus and pine lightly tickle my nose. I look around and zero in on the treadmill. The truth is, I'm not actually your work-out-at-the-gym type. I was just trying to get Stefano to let me out of the room. I don't even know how to use anything here besides the stationary bike and the treadmill.

I climb on and hit the buttons until it turns on.

Stefano gets on the rowing machine and rows like he means business.

Oh damn—those muscles, flexing. Sheer beauty. Something flutters deep in my belly. Seeing the power in that body, the ease with which he uses it makes me remember every time he's touched me. How gentle he's been considering what that body's capable of. I relive every moment of struggling with him in the elevator in the parking garage. The first spanking. The second.

The orgasms he's delivered.

My nipples chafe against the inside of the tank top's shelf bra, hard as diamonds.

I don't know what it is about Stefano Tacone, but the raw animal attraction can't be denied.

So yeah, I guess he can keep me tied up in his room. For at least another day.

He finishes with the rowing machine and works his way around each weight-training station until I'm damp between the thighs and drooling for him. The last station is behind me, but I watch him in the mirror, closing my lips around the sighs that keep trying to slip out.

He finishes and walks right up behind me, stepping on the edges of the treadmill and reaching past me to turn it off. His body is flush against mine, the bulge of his cock hitting my lower back, his beefy arms caging me.

"Think you can just eye-fuck me for an hour without repercussions, *bella*?" He reaches around and cups my mons, pressing the heel of his hand against my clit the same way I do when I'm masturbating. Apparently not satisfied with the full handful he just took, he shifts to slip his hand inside my yoga pants. "*Fanculo*, baby. You're so ripe for me."

I catch sight of my face in the mirror, mouth open, abandon already creeping over my expression. When I realize he's looking, too, I snap my jaw shut, but he plunges a finger inside me.

"Stefano," I pant.

He dips two more fingers in, and I'm already on the edge, about to come. "What, baby?"

"Someone could come in."

"Nah, I locked the doors, beautiful. I'd never let you be seen like that." He pulls his fingers out and yanks my tank top off. "That is, unless you're into being seen. But I don't think you are. Take those pants off."

I obey. Apparently I'm getting used to being stripped naked for him. "What makes you so sure?"

He fishes a condom out of his gym shorts pocket—which means he planned this from the start—and rips it open. Without dropping his shorts, he pulls out his dick and rolls it on, then twirls his finger to tell me to turn back around. "You're proud but you don't seek attention. You like to control how you're seen and when. You're not a submissive." He bends both my arms behind my back and pushes my chest down on the controls for the tread-mill. He leans over, lips at my ear. "But you do like to be tied up and taken hard."

"No, I don't," I insist but he's inching into me. My mouth opens wide again, like a porn star. He retreats, inches in again—taking his sweet time. "Jesus, Stefano, are you ever going to start?"

He chuckles as he pushes in, but then he doesn't move, just reaches around and diddles my clit. His other hand still loosely holds my forearms together at my back.

I arch back against him, desperate to take him deeper, to get satisfaction.

"You know why a woman like you wants to be tied up?"

"Fuck you, Stefano."

"You mean fuck *me*, don't you? Do you need another lesson in begging?"

"No," I pant, need burning into anger, the fever licking between my thighs, up my neck, across my breasts.

He doesn't move.

"Oh God," I moan, already conceding defeat. "Please fuck me. Hard."

"Of course, *bella*. Who would refuse you that?" He palms my breast and pinches my nipple. "Especially when you look so beautiful taking my cock." He draws back and drills into me, hard.

I sigh in relief.

Using my elbows for leverage, he withdraws and slams in, again and again.

"You haven't answered me." Another brutal thrust. My inner thighs quiver. I go up on my tiptoes, thrust my ass back at him. "Do you know why you like to be restrained? And don't say you don't, because I'm inside your sopping pussy right now, baby. I know you're three strokes from an orgasm."

"Ugn." I make an unintelligible sound and then whimper, closing my lids.

"Open your eyes, Corey. I want to see those baby blues in the mirror when I make you come. When I own you so completely you forget your name."

God, it's true. I'm already there.

"Why, Stefano?" I pant because I need to know the answer now. Whatever it is he thinks he knows about me.

"Because letting go of control would be wrong. And you like to get things right, don't you, *amore*?"

I squeeze my eyes shut as pain spears my chest. He got it so right it burns. All my childhood I was made to feel wrong, never good enough. Always a fuck up.

My dad was an exacting bastard who liked to lecture, like to tell me what to do. Liked to slap us around if he was drinking.

The pain of that reality comes slamming through me at the same time as the pleasure of being rode hard by Stefano. I suddenly want to fight him, but it's too late, my body's already capitulated, cunt squeezing around his thick member, pulsing double-time with my heartbeat.

"Fuck," Stefano grunts.

He drags me down to my knees on the sloped treadmill and pushes my torso down. He takes me from this angle until my teeth chatter and my G-spot's numb and then he flips me to my back and finishes, pinning my forearms down to the frame of the treadmill.

I climax with him, hips lifting and bucking against his, my scream loud enough to echo off the mirrors.

I can't move afterward. I'm limp and boneless with the two releases. He'd have to scrape me off the treadmill if he wanted me up.

He gets up and throws his condom away in the trash by the door, which makes me cringe thinking about whoever might see it there.

Then he comes back and leans on the treadmill rail, staring down at me. "I want to keep you naked like this forever. Putting those clothes back on you—as hot as you looked in them—would be a goddamn travesty."

"You got a thing for pasty white skin and birthmarks?" I make fun of myself because I'm feeling too raw, like he stripped me emotionally when he named why I like his form of sex. And I'm starting to enjoy his praise way too much. Believe it, even, which is a huge mistake.

He frowns and shakes his head. "I fucking love that birthmark. I told you that before. I'm going to buy you a whole wardrobe of midriff shirts so you can show it off."

I turn my face away from him, which gets me nowhere since we're surrounded by mirrors.

"Stefano?" I ask the man in the mirror.

"Yeah?"

"What are you going to do with me? For real?"

He walks around to the other side of the treadmill, the side I've turned to and crouches in front of me. His pursed lips are soft and kissable, tangled fingers strong and calloused. "I'm keeping you close. You're going to be my shadow until I'm sure of you."

Relief cascades through me. It must show on my face, because Stefano frowns. "Were you worried I was going to kill you?"

"No," I snap, sitting up, letting my hair curtain my face. For some reason, tears catch in my throat.

Of course he must hear it because he surges around the treadmill and lifts me to my feet, pulling me up against his chest. His free hand brushes lightly over my cheek.

"Then what is it?"

One errant tear leaves my eye and I struggle against him to turn away. I don't even know, myself, why I choked up.

He leans down and flicks it with his tongue. "Is it so awful?" His voice is barely above a whisper.

I find his gaze, surprised. Is it awful? Being Stefano's shadow? His captive prisoner? No. Not at all. He was right; it's wonderful in the *I'm not responsible for any of this so I can let go and enjoy* kind of way.

"I-I think I'm just relieved," I admit.

Stefano's shoulders relax, and he pulls my head against his chest, still holding my wrists captive. "You did still believe I was going to kill you."

The words sound shocking out loud. I'm surprised he can say them so easily, but yes. He's right. Even though he feels like nothing but safety now, some part of me was still scared for my life.

I nod against his chest, hot tears flooding my eyes now.

"That was never my plan," he rumbles above me, his lips in my hair. "I told you that from the beginning."

And I didn't believe you.

He strokes the back of my neck, toying with the baby curls there. "I'm sorry you were afraid, *mi amore*." He kisses my head. "I don't want you afraid of me."

Only at his mercy.

I push away. This still doesn't add up. "And if you can't be sure of me? What then?"

"I'll keep you until I can." He winks. He's trying to tease me, but I'm not having it.

I shake my head. "What if I'm a problem? What then?" I'm pushing for the answer I don't want to hear, but I feel like we need to be clear. He may have treated me to the most incredible sex of my life, but nothing changes what this is. I'm his captive. If I don't cooperate, I'm dead.

He purses his lips. "*Bambina,* what are you trying to get me to say? I don't want to do this."

I put my hands on my hips, challenge clear.

I see the shadow of danger appear on his face. "*Are* you going to be a problem?"

I ignore the twist of fear in my gut. "What if I am?" I whisper, my mouth dry as the Sahara, and I don't mean the casino.

He shoves his hands in his shorts pockets, regards me coolly.

"Then you kill me?" I don't know why this is an argument I'm trying to win. Do I need to prove I have a right to be afraid? That I know what I'm messing with, here?

"No." He shakes his head immediately and takes a step forward, but I step back. He stops. "I told you no already."

"Then what?"

He scrubs a hand across his mouth. "Then I'd use your pressure points," he finally admits.

It's bizarre how much of a relief it is to hear him admit it. To know the score.

"I see. So that's what this is. You tie me to your bed until you're either sure of me, or know enough about me to keep me scared for the rest of my life."

He frowns and lunges for me so quickly I can't dart away. He grabs my arm and pulls me into him, my body tumbling against the hard planes of his large frame. "That's *not* what this is. Don't fucking define it like that." He's mad and I'm not sure why. Oddly, his wrath turns me on.

Does it mean he cares?

Stop it.

RENEE ROSE

Don't think like that. Stefano Tacone doesn't *care* about women. He's a player. He loves women; he takes pleasure in watching women, enjoys their bodies, slakes his lust frequently and with gusto. That doesn't mean he develops feelings for them.

For me.

His lips crash down on mine. I respond before I even start to wonder if I should hold back. It's like my body was made to come alive any time he touches it. It doesn't matter if he was just threatening me, whether he's holding me captive or tormenting me. I'm his.

My pride tells me to push away, but I'm swept up in the moment. I want him to go on, to show me what comes next.

He walks me backward, lips locked until my ass hits a wall, then he keeps pushing, pressing his hard length against my belly as his tongue strokes against mine. He comes up for air and insinuates one solid thigh between my legs. "First of all, I wanted to fuck you the first moment I saw you standing behind that roulette wheel."

Pardon me? I give him a *what the fuck are you talking about* look and he puffs with impatience.

"Were you implying I'm fucking you to keep you quiet? Like I'm some manwhore who solves problems with sex?" He frowns and curses something in Italian.

"If the shoe fits?"

"Well maybe I am, but only with you." His dark gaze bores into me. "*Amore*, you're tangled up in something ugly. Something I never wanted you involved in. It's my fault, and I'm doing my best to fix it."

"Interesting way of fixing it." I can't stop the dryness from crumbling my words.

Stefano picks up my discarded tank and pulls it over my head.

Session over. Discussion ended.

Pretty sure I'm in the same place as when I started, except I have all kinds of happy sex hormones flowing through my veins taking all the bite out of being Stefano's prisoner.

CHAPTER 5

 *tefano*

I TAKE Corey back to the suite, checking my phone for a message from Nico. I haven't heard from him since he called on the way to see our dad in prison, and I'm a little worried. Before we arrive, I get an urgent communication from Tony in the earpiece I'd shoved into my gym shorts pocket.

"We have a situation."

"What is it?" I bark, adjusting the device in my ear.

"Knife wound to one of the guards. A guy stole some lady's purse and he caught him."

"*Fanculo.* Did you call 911?"

Corey shoots me a worried look as the elevator doors open. I grab her elbow and usher her to my suite.

"Emergency vehicle's on the way."

79

"Who's the guard?" I key the door open. An entire rack of clothing for Corey has been delivered while we were gone, but she doesn't move to look at it, she's watching me, listening.

"Joey Spitazzi."

"*Merda*. You call his wife?"

"I'm about to. I'll get her number from HR. What do you want me to do with the bastard who did it?"

"You have him in hand?"

"Oh yeah." There's menace in Tony's voice. He's not a mean guy—doesn't get off on inflicting pain—but he's loyal as hell. And Joey's part of the Family, albeit far removed. He's a grunt, a young soldier. Someone's cousin or other relation who wanted a job from us. Still, he's one of our own. And we protect our own with our lives.

"No, you gotta turn him over to the cops. If an ambulance is coming, authorities will be involved. We can always handle things our own way if we're not happy with how they come out."

"True that. Okay, boss. You want me at the hospital after I talk to the cops?"

"You hold your position here. I'll go to the hospital. Thanks, Tony." I end the call and head into the bedroom to take a quick shower and change back into a suit.

Corey follows me in, standing in the bathroom door as I shuck my clothes, like we're a married couple. "Someone's hurt?"

"Yeah." I climb in the shower and rub a bar of soap quickly over my body. "One of the guards got knifed by a purse-snatcher. I'm going to the hospital."

To my surprise, Corey steps in. As much as I'd love to

drill her against the tile, I don't have time for this shit. But she doesn't look like she's trying to seduce me. "Want me to come along?"

I blink at her, water running down my face. Huh. "Yeah. Okay." Why the fuck not? She might actually make things easier with dealing with the guy's wife. Especially if Joey dies.

Then again, this could be her ploy to escape, and I definitely don't have the bandwidth to keep a leash on her while I'm trying to deal with shit.

She holds her hand out for the bar of soap and I give it to her and step out, my mind already at the hospital, hoping to hell we don't lose a soldier.

Fifteen minutes later, we head down to the parking lot. Corey's wearing an ivory blouse and a pair of black jean capris with her high heels. She looks like a model showing the summer daywear line. I lead her to Nico's black Mercedes and call Tony to find out which hospital Joey was brought to. Twenty minutes later, we enter the waiting area.

A young woman with two preschool-aged children stands up when we get there. Her face is tear-stained and pale, dark hair pulled up in a messy bun on her head. "Nico?" she asks tentatively.

"Stefano Tacone," I say. "Nico's brother."

"I'm Trisha. Joey's wife."

I pull her into an embrace because, well, that's how it's done in my family. A guy takes a knife for you, you're gonna hug his wife, even if you've never met her. "What's the word on Joey?" I ask when we come apart.

Tears pop in her eyes. "He's in surgery. I don't know.

They said even when he comes out, I can't bring the kids back there." Her two little girls hide behind her legs and peek out at us.

"Well, they can stay out here with me," Corey offers. "Or do you have someone who can watch them? I could drop them somewhere."

Relief flickers on Trisha's face. "Yeah, my girlfriend can come when she gets off work, but if I can go see him before then, I need to."

"Of course. I will hang with the kiddos." Corey smiles at the little girls, who stare up at her like she's a princess. And who could blame them? With the heels, Corey stands almost five feet ten inches, and her flame-colored hair cascades in waves down her back like she's royalty. I have to push away the fantasy of wrapping it around my cock and jerking off to it.

"Mommy, I'm hungry," one of the girls says, eyeing Corey, like she's testing to see how sincere she is.

"Let's go find you a snack." Corey holds out her hand.

The little girl shyly takes it.

"Except I'll need Uncle Stefano's wallet because I don't have my purse." She slides me an almost teasing look.

I step to her side and touch her back. It's not that I don't trust she'll come back. I can't see her kidnapping or abandoning a kid. It's that I'm too fascinated by her to want to let her out of my sight. "I'll come along. Where are you headed; the Starbucks down the hall?"

"Yes." She leans down to the look at the little girl. "Think we can find you something there?"

The girl nods gravely. It's a bizarre feeling walking with Corey and a small child through the halls of a hospital. Both new and unique and yet strangely familiar all at once. It would be true of any experience under the sun —with Corey.

She's that different. That right. I never in a million years would've guessed she'd be good with kids. She's not the warm and fuzzy first grade teacher type, yet here she is with a small child wrapped around her finger.

We stand in line at the hospital Starbucks and Corey orders a latte for herself and Trisha and Ninja talks the little girl out of a donut and into a yogurt with fruit. I order a double espresso and drink it before we leave the counter.

"Anything you're not good at, Corey Simonson?" I toss the drained cup in the wastebasket.

Surprise lights up her face. "What are you talking about?"

I lift my chin at the little girl, who is chattering away as she walks beside us, carrying the yogurt and two spoons so she can share with her sister.

Pink stains her cheeks. "I'm not good with kids." She shrugs. "I just figure someone needs to step up right now."

"I read your file. Bachelor in psychology, graduated summa cum laude. Why are you working as a croupier in Vegas?"

She slows her steps, a frown appearing between her brows. "First of all, what file did you read?"

"The one my brother put together when he started dating Sondra. I guess he already knew your dad's a fed."

Her expression clouds even more. "'Kay. I'm a little freaked out now. But maybe no more than I was falling asleep last night with my wrists zip-tied to the bed."

Damn. My concern she'll never forgive me for that seems valid.

She shakes her lovely hair. "Don't respond to that." We arrive back in the waiting area and she hands Trisha the coffee as the girls hunker down together to fight over who gets to hold the yogurt while they share.

Corey takes a seat and I sit beside her, still waiting for an answer. After a moment, she says, "I know it seems like I gave up on my career—my life. My parents definitely think so. I came here for grad school and ended up getting a job at the Bellissimo for shits and giggles. I dropped out three months later."

I knew this much from her file, but I love hearing it from her. I stay quiet, hoping she'll go on.

"The Bellissimo satisfies an itch in me. I always hated the mundane. I get bored quickly, you know?"

I nod, because it makes sense. She's a smart woman— ordinary wouldn't cut it.

"I mean, I grew up in Marshall, Michigan, for God's sake. It's the join the soccer team and mow your grass on Saturdays kind of place. Only I always knew I didn't fit in. I had a dad who worked for the FBI for one thing. And for another, he was a functioning alcoholic and an asshole. Tragically, I probably get my impatience with the rest of the population from him. He was always tearing everyone down. He saw through every lie, destroyed every dream."

She laughs, but it's bitter and I already want to kill her dad. It wouldn't be hard to do.

"Sondra and her family lived across the street—the model of what a family should look like. Cheesy, supportive parents, report cards pinned on the fridge."

She stares down at her fingernails, the low-key French manicure making her fingers look even longer. "Sondra's parents used to come to her soccer games with their faces painted in the team colors. They carried banners and signs cheering her on.

"I always prayed my dad wouldn't come because he would stand on the sidelines and chew me out for every wrong move. He chewed the coach out, the other team's coach. The other kids. It was a freaking nightmare."

"Father of the year," I mutter.

"Yeah." She jerks her head up suddenly to look at my eyes. "Why am I even telling you all this?"

"You were explaining how you came to be a croupier."

"Right." She sighs and stares across the waiting area at the exit. "Why I hate normal. So yeah, I have a degree in psych because I'm interested in people. What makes them tick. But school was too ordinary, too boring. Too structured and delineated and confining. So I figured why learn from a textbook when I can study the Bellissimo clientele to my heart's delight? And the money's good."

Something inside my chest rearranges. I can't quite name the clawing need rising up. A desire to fix her pain? Protect her from more of it? Free her from all the bullshit of life? As if that could be done. No, life's a shithole for most everybody. A few people rise above because they have that raw potency the rest of the population foregoes. I think that may actually be what Corey's talking about with her rejection of normal. She's not going to lie down and take it. She's fighting back, even if being a croupier seems like she laid down to take it to the rest of the world.

"You ever think about going back?"

"To school?" She raises her eyebrows. "Nah. I often think I *should*. I won't have any career to fall back on when my boss fires me for calling him an asshole one too many times." She darts a glance under her lashes at me that makes my dick twitch in my pants. I might have been wrong about her not being submissive under all the bluster. "Or if I break my ankle and can't stand behind the table for hours on end. Or when I get bored with categorizing gamblers. But I really can't get myself excited about it. Up until I dropped out of grad school I was still trying to prove my worth to my dad, who never saw it. And now that I finally realized my idiocy, I just can't make myself do things that conventional wisdom says I *should* do." She shrugs. "I don't want to be ordinary."

Corey

OH SHIT. What in the hell made me overshare like this?

Stefano stares at me, his dark, curling lashes thick and beautiful against the backdrop of such a masculine face. I can't read him, but his attention makes me shift in my seat, change the crossing of my legs.

A nurse comes out and calls for Trisha. We all stand up and watch as Trisha rushes over. When she returns, she says, "They said he came out of surgery and is stable. He probably won't wake up tonight, so she said I should go home to rest and come back tomorrow." Her lip trembles.

Stefano reaches in his pocket and produces a business

card. "My cell number's on there. Keep me posted, all right?"

She bobs her head, eyes filling with tears. "Yeah, okay. I will. Thanks so much."

He touches her shoulder. "The Bellissimo will take care of all the medical expenses and missed pay. All Joey needs to worry about is recovering."

Trisha surges forward and gives him a tight hug around his waist.

Stefano one-arm hugs her back. As we walk away, he interlaces his fingers with mine. My breath stalls a moment. After all the things he's done to me—we've done together—it's odd that holding my hand is the gesture that feels most intimate, but it does.

It's tender. Sweet.

Things I don't associate with Stefano Tacone, royalty to the Vegas underworld.

I can't even imagine why he'd do it, and yet it also feels perfect. Exhilarating, even.

On the ride back, he calls into the casino for a report and lets them know the status of Joey.

I arrive back at the Bellissimo a changed woman. It's like I'm seeing things for the first time as I glide in with Stefano's hand on my lower back. Seeing them from his perspective, realizing how much he has to worry about with Nico gone.

And yet he doesn't ditch me straightaway, as I expected. I wasn't even going to complain. No, he asks me which restaurant in the casino is my favorite.

"Caffe Milano," I tell him, indicating the eatery modeled after a Italian sidewalk cafe. It has cute little tables nestled together and sprawling outside the restaurant in a lush patio. "They have the best Caprese salad."

His lips twitch and he leads me there, requesting the table out on the "sidewalk"—which really just means outside the pseudo-enclosure, with a view of the casino hustle and bustle.

"Is this so you can keep an eye on things?" I ask as he holds my chair for me.

"Yes. You keep an eye out, too."

I love that he recruits me like this, the way he did last night on the floor before the ill-fated game. He thinks I might have something to contribute to his efforts. It makes me want to please him, which is probably dangerous territory. I don't need to be working hard to impress a guy. I did that way too long with my dad. But maybe I purposely chose a loser like Dean because I didn't want to have to impress a guy.

"Tell me about the categories you put gamblers in." Stefano shifts his gaze from the passersby to me.

I curse the flush that hits my cheeks. Why did I ever tell him so much?

"Come on, don't be shy." He pours more wine in my glass. "I want to hear what you've learned. It could be useful for me working security."

I tilt my head to the side. "Yeah, it probably could. It's how I knew something was off with you that first night."

His sensual lips spread into a slow grin. He leans forward, eyes glittering with intensity. "Tell me."

I'd like to say I'm immune to having my every word hung onto by a sexy, powerful man, but it does something crazy to my insides. My nipples harden, but it's beyond sexual. It's more like energy swirling around me, whispering dangerous things in my ear. Things I want to believe.

I take a sip of wine. His attention remains riveted on me. "There's three kinds of big gamblers," I tell him. "The cerebral, the wild and crazy and the energetic, for lack of a better term." I go on to explain each one and he hangs onto my every word.

"And so if someone's spending big and he or she isn't one of these three, you know something's off."

I nod. "Right. And I should've known last night because Donahue didn't fit, either. I had a lot of signs things were off with him, but I didn't put it together fast enough."

Stefano covers my hand with his. "I'm sorry you had to see that. I really am."

I don't want to contemplate what it means that he didn't say he was sorry it happened, or sorry a guy's dead or any of that. I mean, I would've done the same thing in his shoes. The guy was going to kill him. But he's taken it all pretty coolly.

His comms unit buzzes and he listens and speaks into it. Then he looks at our empty plates. "I need to get out on the floor. You want to come with me? Be my shadow for the night?"

It's a Stockholm Syndrome sign that I get excited by his offer, as if he's taking me out on the town for a fancy date, rather than letting me out of his room. Still, I nod eagerly, because it's what I want.

"Let me see you in one of those dresses they brought

up to my room, then." He stands up and leads me to the elevator.

I ignore the fact that there's a little thrill at the idea of dressing for him, providing the visual stimulation he was looking for when he asked me to work the private games.

"So are you going to let me back on the floor, or am I still your private game dealer?" I ask in the elevator. What I'm really asking is—will my imprisonment ever end? Will I still have a job? When can we get back on familiar ground so I can recover from this insane ride?

He considers me. "I'm not sure, *amore*. What's your preference?"

"Back on the floor," I say without hesitation.

He nods. "Where you can observe the masses?"

"Exactly."

He shrugs his shoulders. "I think you're meant for more, *bella*. Your skill set goes way beyond flipping cards and counting chips, although you're damn good at it."

And just like that he upsets my cart—the stroke of my ego making me almost miss the fact that he's refusing my choice again.

His cell phone rings and something akin to relief flickers over his face. "Nico," he answers, "What the fuck?"

I hear Nico say something about his phone being dead.

"How'd it go?" Stefano asks in a low, serious tone.

We're in the suite now, but I don't move, wanting to hear. Stefano slaps my ass and lifts a chin at the rack of clothing. I scowl at him, but move away. For all I know, they're discussing something illegal. Lord knows I don't need to be implicated in any more crimes.

The clothes Stefano had sent up must cost a fortune.

They're from one of the casino's luxury shops—a place for high-rollers to spend their winnings. It's all high-fashion couture, brand names and they make me look like a million bucks. Too bad I don't get to keep them.

As I change into one of the red dresses—a close-fitting dress with a strip of fabric around the neck, but a cutout across my chest to show off my cleavage—I hear Stefano curse in Italian. "And Sondra? She okay?"

I stand in the doorway to listen and Stefano doesn't shoo me away.

"Thank fuck," he says, which I take to mean that Sondra's okay. Does Stefano's relief indicate she almost wasn't? He listens for another minute, then says, "All right, I'll see you tomorrow. Looking forward to meeting my future sister-in-law." He winks at me, but the line between his brows make his expression appear serious. He ends the call and walks over to me, touching my waist. "It fits. Christ, you're beautiful." He brushes my hair back from my shoulder and bites my neck.

"Yeah, this one will do as my replacement dress."

"Keep all of them." He waves his hand dismissively. I'm not sure if he realizes that rack probably encompasses over 10K in clothing. "Nobody should wear a red dress but you. You're a fucking knock-out in red."

I snort. "Don't you know redheads aren't supposed to wear red?" I'm already calculating how much I can make selling them on Ebay.

"Oh, I know. But you're no *ordinary* redhead." He emphasizes the word *ordinary* like he really heard me earlier, really gets what I meant. And I realize I'll never sell a single one.

"What happened with Nico and Sondra?" I demand.

Stefano shakes his head. "Just some shit Nico had to work out."

"About getting out of his marriage contract?"

Stefano arches a brow. "You know about that?"

I put my hands on my hips. "I told you I'm practically family."

He grins. "So you are." He rubs his shadowed jaw. "Nico fixed it. Our brother made him sweat it, though. They scared the hell out of your cousin, but she's fine. I would apologize, but if I took responsibility for the nasty things my family does, I'd never stop."

My heart squeezes a little for Stefano. Like me, he can't help who his father is. He hasn't escaped the legacy of violence.

His comms unit buzzes again. "Let's move, *bella*. We've got shit to do."

CHAPTER 6

 *tefano*

I WALK around the casino with Corey at my side. People who don't recognize her assume she's my girlfriend. I'm sure we make a striking pair. Those who do know her, shoot her a range of stares, varying from jealous to concerned to bald curiosity.

On the way down, she complained about not having any cosmetics, so we stopped at the salon to have her makeup done, and then I had to take her to the in-house jeweler to buy a pair of diamond drop earrings.

I like spoiling her. The fact that Corey doesn't gush or purr when I do makes it all the more pleasurable. She plays hard to get, making me work for her smiles and make up for keeping her as my captive. But it's not just about the chase with her.

I'm fucking fascinated.

But I'd have to be out of my mind to get seriously involved with the daughter of a fed. A *crooked* fed, according to Nico's research. Which means an unpredictable, dangerous asshole. And Junior, my asshole brother who just put a gun to Nico's head for wanting to marry the woman of his choosing, would probably order me to off the guy if I wanted to keep seeing Corey.

And I'm not going to kill her fucking father. Even if they are estranged.

I lean into Corey. We're observing one of the blackjack tables, making the croupier nervous. "Tell me about who you see," I murmur.

"Cerebral spender. Probably trying to count cards. When he loses count, he runs his hand through his hair and shakes the ice in his drink. Which he hasn't drunk a drop from."

"Working alone?"

"Yes. He's up two thousand, but he's getting tired. The stress of it wears him out."

I stroke my hand up and down Corey's side. Being near her body electrifies me, but hearing how her brain works—witnessing her brilliance firsthand—that sets my soul on fire.

"What else?" I prompt.

"Jack is the croupier. He accidentally put a $20 chip meant for him in the house pot, probably because we're freaking him out watching. Otherwise, he's a decent dealer."

"Anyone else interesting?"

"Nah. Young people who don't know what they're doing. People with money to lose. That's it."

"Next table." I guide her to another perch and order her a drink. The floor manager comes over to check in and when he's gone, she gives me an equally germane report on the three tables in her view.

If she were a beefy man, I would put her on my security team in a heartbeat. As it is, I can't decide the best use of her incredible talents. "I'm thinking I want you on every employment interview at the Bellissimo. You sure you don't want a job in HR?"

She wrinkles her nose at me.

Another idea strikes me. "Do you ever play poker, yourself?"

She changes the crossing of her long legs and memories of those legs spread on my bed gets me hard. It's a perpetual state around this woman. "Croupiers aren't allowed to gamble in their own casino."

I grin. "You telling me the rules now, smarty-pants? I mean elsewhere."

She shakes her head, but I watch something come to life in her. "I've always wanted to. I actually love to watch those championships; the ones that are televised on the sports channel? I swear to God, I could beat those guys. I'm serious; if I had money to burn, I'd totally enter."

I sit back, satisfied. Corey Simonson just confessed something she wants in life.

I'll be damned if I don't make it happen.

Tony calls my cell at the same time Leo buzzes through the comms unit and the floor manager walks over with a whale he wants to introduce me to.

"Excuse me." Corey slides off the barstool. "I'm going to the restroom."

I nod distractedly and take care of all the issues at hand before I get that niggling feeling about Corey choosing that moment to excuse herself. I glance at the nearest restroom. She should've been back by now.

Fuck.

Well, if she was making a run for it, there's a good chance she'd go to her locker to get her purse with her keys and phone. I walk briskly in that direction. As I round the corner, I see her leaving the employee locker room, heading for the nearest exit.

Sonofabitch.

Corey

I'M ALMOST at the door when two beefy Guido security guards charge toward me from opposite directions. I break into a run. One of them lunges for me, and catches my arm, his iron grip bruising.

"Boss says don't touch her," the other relays with a note of panic in his voice.

The guy releases me like I'm a hot potato but they both jockey to block my exit. It's almost comical, like some birthday party game where you can't use your hands to pass an egg to your partner.

I use their abject fear of Stefano's wrath to my advantage and knee the guy in front of me in the balls. He goes over with a groan, clutching the family jewels. Yes. I'm at Knee-2, Balls-0.

"*Corey.*" Stefano's censuring bark comes from a few feet behind me.

I try to dart around the other guard, but Stefano catches my arm and yanks me back. The room spins as I'm upended over his shoulder like a sack of potatoes.

"Stefano," I protest as he carries me swiftly toward the bank of elevators. "You're making a scene."

"No, you made the scene, *bella.*" He hits the elevator button. "And you'll suffer the consequences." I'm glad he sounds so cool, calm and collected, because I'm trying to fight back panic over what he's going to do to me. What will the *consequences* be?

He gets in the elevator and flashes his ID to get to his suite level. The doors swish closed. Another couple is in the elevator, snickering over my predicament.

"*Stefano.*"

I really want him to put me down.

"Corey."

The young woman giggles, whispering to her partner. It feels like ages before the elevator stops and they get off. Someone else tries to get on, but Stefano clips, "Wait for the next one," and hits the door close button.

Thank God.

When we get to his floor, he carries me off and still he doesn't put me down. His movements are smooth and assured, like he always manages to open and close doors one-handed with a woman over his shoulder.

He carries me toward the kitchen where he opens a drawer and produces a roll of duct tape.

Oh shit.

Now I go down on my feet, but he maintains control of my body, pinning my hands to the wall and taping them down with a long strip of duct tape. He reinforces it with three more strips, then pulls my hips back and kicks my legs open. His intention is clear; my ass is out and presented. I'm going to get spanked again.

I should *not* be excited.

I'm freaking thrilled.

He leaves and returns with a pair of scissors.

"Again?" I complain. "You could just strip me before you tape my hands down next time. Ever think of that?"

"You are in no position to get smart with me, *amore*."

I believe him. He's definitely all business right now. I see none of the hot passion that sometimes motivates him. Nor any trace of bemusement.

At least he doesn't seem angry, although maybe he's just not the angry type.

The dress falls away in pieces and he uses the scissors to remove my bra and panties as well.

"You could've just taken those off," I grumble.

"I could have," he says, almost cheerfully. "But I wanted to cut them. I might not be so quick to replace your things this time, either."

My pussy clenches at the thought of him keeping me taped to his wall, naked, for days.

I shake my head to erase the thought. I'm fuck-nuts crazy.

Stefano walks to the balcony door and fiddles with the curtain. At first I think he's going to draw them closed, but when he turns, he's detached the plastic rod used to pull them. He whacks it in his palm and I freak out.

I yank on my hands, trying to pull them off the wall, but they won't budge.

"*Tsk tsk.* You're not going anywhere, *bella*. Your ass is mine right now, and I'm not going easy on it."

"Stefano." I curse the waver in my voice. I also curse the wetness between my legs. Why on earth would the idea of being whipped with a curtain rod excite me?

"Legs apart. Ass out. Hold the position like a good girl and I'll consider lightening your sentence."

Oh shit. I am so in over my head.

I do as I'm told, because what's the alternative? I'm in no position to argue, and it could only get worse from here. I widen my stance and hollow my back to present my ass to him.

He taps it with the makeshift cane. "Good girl. I won't make you count. You can focus on breathing and holding your position." He swings the implement through the air.

I hear the displacement of air a moment before it strikes and I scream like I'm in a horror film.

Stefano's at my back, a hand wrapped around my mouth to stifle the sound. "Shh, bambina. No screaming. It's bad for business." He steps away.

I'm not so brave this time. I twist my ass away from him, hanging from the bonds with all my weight.

"That's cute, *bambina*, but I asked you to stay in position."

Fuck.

He sure did.

I reluctantly put myself back in the humiliating pose.

Stefano swings the cane again and a second line of pure fire blooms directly beneath the first.

I choke on my cry.

"Hold still." Stefano's tone is sharp, like he's run out of patience with me. Regrettably, it has the effect of freezing me in position.

He whips me again, and again, neat even lines down my ass that leave me moaning and trembling. Six in all.

And then he's on his knees behind me, prying my twitching cheeks apart and licking a line from my pussy to anus.

I can barely stand, my legs are so shaky and weak, but it doesn't matter, the duct tape holds me up against the wall. Stefano moves in front of me and he goes to town on my pussy. His strong hands hold my thighs as he sucks and nips my labia, flicks his tongue over my clit. A moment ago, he was my stern master, punishing me for my disobedience. Now he's a servant, worshipping between my legs. He devours me like my taste is his ambrosia, like he's dying of hunger and only my pussy will satisfy.

The burning, throbbing pain becomes only intensity as my flesh swells and blossoms under his ministrations.

"Stefano," I moan, my hips dancing above him. I won't last much longer, and he's not even using his fingers to penetrate me.

He increases his fervor, the stubble on his chin scraping my inner thighs as he works me over.

Stars dance before my eyes and my head swims like I'm going to pass out.

"Stefano!" I scream again, and then I crest the peak,

tumbling over the other side into pleasure, release, pleasure.

My pussy clenches on air, spasming around nothing. It's both satisfying and not enough. I want his cock in me.

And then I'm too weak to stand, falling against the wall, against his body as he kisses my pussy reverentially.

Stefano

I LOVE the sound of Corey calling out my name just before she comes.

This time *I'm* the one who feels like crying afterward.

Not that I know what it is to cry. I had that urge beat out of me before I hit the ripe age of six. But my throat and face are tight with what can only be described as sorrow.

I'm wrung out. Maybe it's guilt from the whipping I gave her. Maybe I can't stand that she tried to leave me.

I rise slowly, barely fitting between the wall and Corey's body. I cup her face. "What am I going to do with you?" I ask sadly.

She nuzzles her face against my hand. Her head's lolling like her neck can't work to hold it up.

I peer up at her hands and reach behind myself to pry the tape off. Then I tug her to a chair and pull her onto my lap. She comes willingly, leaning her head back on my shoulder as I caress her bare breasts, her inner thighs.

"Why did you leave, Corey?" I have to ask it. It's

fucking killing me. Is she still afraid of me? Does she really still think I'm going to kill her?

"I don't know," she sighs. "It's just... too intense. I can't stay here locked up with you like this. I'm losing myself."

My heart stops beating. Then restarts at a jauntier pace. She isn't afraid of me. She's afraid of *us*.

Fuck, so am I, baby. So am I.

"I'm losing myself, too," I admit, kissing her jaw, her slender neck. "But only cowards run."

Corey chokes on a laugh and I smile, too.

"Come on, *bambina*. We'd better get something on your ass before you bruise. I know how delicate redheads are."

I scoop her into my arms and carry her to the bedroom, where I arrange her on her belly. She's docile as a child now, but a good whipping and orgasm will do that to a woman.

I search in my bathroom for a salve my cousin in Sicily made me and return.

Corey hasn't moved. She lies prone with her face hidden in the bedspread. My heart shoots into my throat. Is she crying?

I stroke her hair back from her face, and my shoulders ease. Her expression is soft, relaxed. Almost blissful.

Thank fuck.

I take an ample amount of salve and rub it over the cane marks, working it into her skin.

"What is that?"

"It's a salve I brought back from Sicily. Helps with bruising."

"There's a salve for bruising?"

"I got it from my cousin. She makes a salve for just

about everything. She's one of those natural healing types —you know, into essential oils and herbs."

"And she gave it to you because you have a propensity for getting bruises or *giving* bruises?" Her dry question gets under my skin.

I screw the lid back on the salve and drop it onto the bed. "Why do you have to keep poking that wound, baby? You need to remind me I'm no good for you? That you're better than me?"

"*What?* No." She rolls over and props herself up on an elbow, a line folding between her brows.

"I know, I know. I'm the bad guy. I'm on the wrong side of the law and your father's on the right side."

Corey goes pale. "My dad definitely isn't the good guy. Not by any means." Her words come out rough.

I'm instantly sorry. She told me they weren't on speaking terms. Now I'm the one poking wounds. I sink down beside her. "Yeah, neither is mine," I admit.

To my surprise, her fingers seek out my hand and she curls them over it and squeezes. I stare down at our interlocked fingers. When's the last time any woman offered me comfort? When's the last time I *let* her?

Oh yeah, never.

But this woman's different. Everything's so raw between us. It's the intensity she mentioned—why she had to bail.

But I'm not letting her.

My phone buzzes again and I almost lose patience with it. "What?" I snap.

"We have a situation down here," Tony says in a low voice.

Fuck. What now?

I lean over and kiss Corey's shoulder. "Tell me you'll still be in my bed when I get back?"

I see the understanding flare in her eyes. I'm letting her go. Maybe it's guilt over punishing her, maybe it's that I want to reward her honesty. Or it's just time; I don't know.

She nods and I pull the covers back to help her in. I kiss her lips this time, softly. "Good. I'll see you in the morning, then."

"Yeah. See you."

I start to leave, then turn back. "You need anything? Room service? A drink? Ibuprofen?"

"No, I'm going to sleep," she says. "Come back soon."

And that's when I know I'm fucked. Because the little backflip my heart does at those words is nothing I've ever experienced before.

CHAPTER 7

 orey

I HEAR Stefano come in around 4:00 a.m. but I fall right back to sleep. I wake later to him palming my breast, teasing the nipple as his cock lurches against my ass. I'm still naked from our escapades the night before. And of course, he never got off. I'm surprised he let me sleep this long.

I turn and push him to his back, then climb over him to straddle his waist. His eyes darken as his cock tents his boxer briefs. I free it, moisten the head with my tongue.

He groans. "I give you thirty seconds to tease. Then I'm going to flip you on your back and pound you into oblivion."

My pussy clenches at the threat. "Oh yeah?" I slide my

lips over his cock, taking him deeper as my fist works the base. His hips jack up and he thrusts into my mouth.

"Fuck, *bambina*. See what I mean?" He reaches for my head, and then, as if to keep himself from forcing me down on him, fists his hands in the air. Then he opens them and tears at his own hair instead.

I hum softly around his member, swirl my tongue on the underside as I pull out. A few drops of his salty essence rewards my efforts. I suck harder, hollowing my cheeks as I pull away.

Stefano growls and wraps a fist in my hair. "Fuck, yeah, baby. Take me deeper."

I do. I take him as deep as I can go, slowing down so I don't trigger my gag reflex.

"*Bella, bella donna*," he croons.

His breathing grows short, he starts using my hair to tug me down over him faster, deeper, thrusting up at the same time. "Enough. Enough." He pulls me off, his lip curling like the strain of holding back is killing him. "Roll over. Spread those legs."

I lay on my belly and spread my legs wide. He swipes his fingers over my wetness and puts them in his mouth. "You taste so good, Corey." He goes to the closet and returns with condoms and a bottle of lube. I didn't think I needed lube, but I have to defer. Stefano is definitely a sex god. He must have some plan.

He snaps on a condom and pulls my hips up until I'm on my knees, then eases into me at the same time he reaches around and rubs my clit.

I push back to take him, shivering on a long inhale through my teeth.

Stefano stops, buried in me and plays with my nipples. "You good?"

"I'm good," I moan, arching my back. "Go on."

He chuckles and tweaks my nipple a bit harder before he grips my hips and uses me the way I was hoping he would. Deeper and deeper he thrusts, my hips on the perfect angle to take his full length.

I'm on a rocket ship headed for the moon when he squirts lube onto my anus and starts rubbing it in.

I gasp, trying to tuck my tail and pull away, but he won't have it. With a few quick twists, he's sunk his thumb into my ass. His other fingers splay across my back, and I'm owned completely. The twin sensations, double penetrations spin me out into hedonistic pleasure —total sensation, vulgar and satisfying.

I start making guttural vocalizations, panting into the bed, my eyes rolling back in my head.

He starts making tiny thrusts with his thumb that match the thrusts of his cock, locking me into surrender.

I can't even speak to moan his name. I'm lost. Shattering, coming together. He rides me, handles me. His movements are sure and commanding.

"Uhn, uhn, uhn," I moan with each brutal thrust.

"Take it, *bella*. Take it like a good girl."

"Yes," I gasp.

He pounds even harder.

I whine.

"Come now," he roars and thrusts three more times before he thrusts deep and stays, pistoning his thumb in and out as my pussy grabs and releases his cock in quick bursts.

I sob with the release, utterly spent. The room spins, I can't see a thing. Oh yeah, that's because my eyes are closed and my face is in the sheets.

After a moment, awareness returns. Stefano returns from the bathroom with a washcloth, which he uses to clean me up.

Then he applies more salve on my ass and settles down beside me, kissing my shoulder.

~

Stefano

"Nico and your cousin come back today."

I don't know why I say it. I mean, I know she wants that information, which I got from Nico when he called late last night, but it's a piss-poor moment to share it. But I feel the weight of what I've done to Corey settle too heavily on my shoulders.

I have to let her go today. Release her to her life. Keeping her prisoner forever wasn't a solid plan.

"Yeah?" Corey pushes up on her forearm, her pretty breasts shifting to hang sideways. I cup the lower one and run my thumb over the nipple. Such sweet, perfect-sized breasts.

"I'm looking forward to meeting the woman who stole my brother's heart." There's no lightness behind the words, even though it's true. I'm trying to control the caveman part of me that's stomping in a circle around my mind, demanding I tie her back up and never set her free.

I go for honestly.

"I want to keep you chained naked in my bedroom for the rest of my life, *bella*."

"But?" She already knows what's coming.

"But I'd prefer it be voluntary."

Her lips twitch once and then stretch into a full smile. "It's a bit late to ask for consent, my friend."

"I know. But I want you to stay."

She drops her gaze and I already know the answer she'll give. "I gotta get back to my place." She says it like she's sorry, but the words fall flat. She doesn't even offer up a reason, and I'm not going to push.

This is what she wants.

I purse my lips and nod. "I expect you back here at 8:00 p.m. for your shift."

Wariness flickers over her expression. "Private game?"

"No. Casino floor. Where you want to be."

I'm trying to give her something, but she only appears sad about it.

"I'll be here," she says, and pushes herself up to sit.

I sigh. "You can shower first. I'll order room service. What do you want for breakfast?"

"Bacon and fruit. Too bad they don't do Starbucks drinks for room service."

"I can hook you up. What's your drink?"

"Grande latte, hot?"

"You bet." I get up and dial the front desk to send a bellhop over to the in-house Starbucks for me, then call room service. At least I can do this one small thing for her.

And she's coming back.

In less than twelve hours she'll be back in the Bellissimo. Calling me boss.

Things could be worse.

CHAPTER 8

 orey

THE MOMENT I GET HOME, I can't figure out what my hurry was. I hate my place. This is the stupid apartment I shared with Dean, after all. The lecherous asshole loser I picked. I can't even remember what I saw in him. I guess he let me live small. Slow myself down. His lack of ambition made my life choices shiny in comparison.

It's no surprise I returned to my place totally changed. It's like when you go on vacation and when you come back, you see things through fresh eyes, at least for your first day back. I've been living in the Bellissimo with Stefano Tacone for the past forty-eight hours. The second-hand furniture in my apartment now appears dingy and sad. The stained carpet moans to be replaced and nothing in the place even represents me.

111

Have I even been living a life here?

What was it?

I don't know who the fuck I am.

No, that's not true. I'm just exhausted. I was a *prisoner* for the past forty-eight hours. Except I know that's not really true.

I may have stripes on my ass that says it is, but it's not.

Or maybe it is, but I was a *most honored* prisoner. I mean truthfully? Stefano Tacone—for all his power and fearsome capabilities, for all the mighty control he flexed —treated me better than Dean ever did. And Dean never raised a hand to me.

I had the best orgasms of my life. I ate good food and drank expensive wine. I came home with thousands of dollars worth of clothing, carried to my car by a most attentive bellhop. I'm still wearing twelve hundred dollar diamond earrings.

But I'd be a fool if I attached any meaning to any of it.

Stefano is a player. Fucking women and showering them with parting gifts is probably par for the course for him.

The doorbell of my townhouse rings and I frown. I'm not expecting anyone. I open the door a crack and look out. A large man in a suit immediately pushes it open and my stomach bunches up to the size of a nut.

It tightens so much it hurts, because the man pushing into my apartment is the *last* man I want to see on a normal day. But I especially don't want to see him today.

It's my goddamn dad.

Shit.

"Hey, Corey." His slow drawl belies the aggressive way he entered. "Is that any way to greet your dear old dad?"

I can't dignify that with an answer. I cross my arms over my chest. "What are you doing here?"

He walks around my place, his critical gaze probably cataloguing everything he sees to use against me in some way. "I've been transferred to Las Vegas."

Fuck.

"I'm working a possible murder case. Turns out my own daughter might know something about it."

My heart's in tachycardia but I curl my lip in a sneer. "How do you figure?"

"I heard you're the dealer for the private games now."

Now my heart stops. How in the fuck does he know this? How? Has he been casing out the Bellissimo this whole time? The Tacones?

Jesus, he's going to get me killed! Me and Sondra both.

"A man named Eric Donahue disappeared after attending a private game Saturday night. Were you dealing that game?"

I can't believe Stefano didn't go over alibis with me. Tell me what to say if I'm ever questioned. I'm a freaking accessory to murder, and there's no way my dad won't see through a lie. He's a seasoned federal agent. And he's my father.

I cross my arms over my chest. "I'm not discussing anything with you. You're not welcome in my home, and I need you to leave. Now."

My father doesn't move from where his ass is perched against the arm of the couch. He studies me with gray eyes.

113

Yeah, I just confirmed everything for him. Whatever he wanted to know, he knows it now.

I'm so fucked.

"I'm sure you don't want to be uncooperative with a federal investigation."

"I'm sure I do if it's led by you."

"Okay, what is your problem, really? I didn't call enough after I moved to Detroit? Didn't pay for your college education?"

"I don't have a problem. I just don't want you in my life. It's quite simple, really."

He stands and walks toward me, spreading his arms like he wants to hug me. "Corey, what is this all about? I never understood why you stopped talking to me."

"I grew up, Dad. That's why. I grew up and realized you were a shitty dad, and I didn't want to have a relationship with you. It's not that hard to understand. Aren't you supposed to be a member of Mensa or something?"

"So are you," he murmurs. "Maybe we're just too similar."

"Or maybe it's because you're a bully and you cheated on Mom and all you ever did was shove your judgments down my throat." I'm getting myself worked up and—*fuck!*—I hate when I lose my temper. Especially because it *does* make me just like him.

"*Out,*" I snap, pointing to the door.

He shakes his head like he pities me. "Getting involved with the Tacones is a big mistake."

My nostrils flare. Of course, every word of this upcoming speech is predictable, but I still can't stand hearing it.

"I heard about Sondra's engagement. Big. Mistake."

"Yeah, well no one asked your opinion."

"Her father did," he corrects me.

Ugh. That sucks. Sondra doesn't need the stress of having her parents oppose her marriage after talking to my dad.

"Nico Tacone will never hurt Sondra." That was more than I wanted to blurt. I don't need to convince him of what I needed convincing of myself. He doesn't deserve a say in this. I sure as hell hope he's not invited to the wedding.

I make a mental note to talk to Sondra about that. I'm sure she'll agree, seeing as how her future husband could be harrassed by my dad.

"Yeah, I'm sure," my dad drawls dryly.

"I told you to get out. I'm not discussing this or any other part of my life with you further. Don't come back."

He pulls an amused face, like I'm a silly toddler but saunters for the door.

Thank God.

I hold my breath until he shuts the door behind himself. Even then, I don't know how long it takes me before I exhale. But as soon as I do, my stomach scrunches up under my ribs again.

What if Stefano's having me watched to make sure I don't talk about what happened? What if I just proved his suspicions about me are true?

I'm so fucked.

Stefano

"*FANCULO.* YOU LOOK LIKE SHIT."

Nico's face is covered in bruises, his lip's split and one eye is swollen shut. He texted me to say he's back and to meet him in his office. I can see why he's hiding up here instead of being out on the floor.

I make a mental note to bring him that salve from Lucia.

"Junior is such a *testa di cazzo*," I mutter as we give each other a back-slapping hug.

Nico shrugs like getting beat to a pulp by your own brother is no big deal. Which to us, it really isn't, considering how we were raised. "It's done. Settled. We're getting married in a month back in Chicago and the whole fucking lot can show up to kiss my ass."

"He just had to show you he's still boss, eh? Even though you're the Tacone who brings in the real dough? Who makes their shit legit?"

"The order came from Pops. Junior picked us up as soon as I hit Chicago. Whatever. I had to pay for defying orders. Now it's done."

I sprawl in one of the comfortable leather armchairs and prop my ankle over one knee.

"So tell me," Nico says.

"Tony didn't already fill you in?" I ask but didn't wait for his response before continuing. "His name was Eric Donahue. Junior says Pops strong-armed his brother out of his restaurant five or six years ago. The guy committed suicide not long after. Seems like this was a revenge attempt. Not sure why he wanted you, but I'm guessing it's because your name's in the press. Like you were easier to look up and find in a public place. So he shows up and finds out how to get a private audience with you. And when he finds out you're not here, but your brother is, I'm just as good a target."

Nico rubs his head. "*Cazzo*. You couldn't make this wash out clean?"

"There was a connection to Pops. Nothing's ever clean there, and when that shit shows up here in your casino? Fuck, yeah, I'm going to make it disappear. What would you have done different?"

Nico taps his desk, then shakes his head. "Nothing. You're right. I just don't want any kind of investigation here."

"I know."

"And the rest of it? What the hell are you doing with Corey?"

"I was keeping an eye on her. Until I could be sure. Her dad's a fed, you know."

"Yeah, I fucking know." He gives me a searching look. "You fuck her?"

"Yeah." I raise the end of the syllable like it's a question. Like, why the fuck does it matter what I did with her?

He continues studying me. We're tight, me and Nico. If anyone knows me, it's him. I don't know what the fuck he's seeing now, because I don't even know what I think about the Corey situation. "What do I need to know?"

"Nothing."

He won't drop it. Apparently, he still sees something. "You trust her now?"

I nod. "Yeah. But I got into her phone records and put a guy on her, just to be sure. The situation with her dad could be a pain in the ass."

Nico tips his head to the side. "You have a thing for her?"

Not sure how he got that from me putting a guy on her. "Yeah," I admit.

"You getting anywhere with that?" There's doubt in Nico's voice and I laugh, because he must know Corey's a tough nut to crack. I don't ever fail with women. Maybe that's part of the attraction.

"I'm working it, still." I spread my hands. "What about you? Where is Sondra? I want to meet my new sister-in-law."

Nico smirks and it's nice to see a smile on his face. My brother's been wound tight for as long as I can remember. He definitely seems different now, underneath the bruises.

"Come on, she's in her office." He leads me out.

"Ah, she works for you." Why hadn't anyone told me that?

"Yes."

"Yes? That's it? What does she do?" When he doesn't go on, I make an impatient *tell me more* motion.

"Sondra is curating the art wing in the Bellissimo. We can display all those masterpieces we've acquired from the whales over the years."

Huh. Not a bad idea. When big gamblers get desperate, they start putting up all kinds of treasures: keys to their cars, vacation properties, and often the priceless art hanging on their walls. We take anything here and we always collect. Which means we have dozens of paintings by famous artists in our vault.

We get off the elevator and Nico leads me to a wing that had been previously used as additional conference area and I see it's been transformed into a gallery.

"Very nice," I murmur, looking around at the beginnings of intricate security systems designed to protect the masterpieces that have not yet been placed. The placards are there, though. Titles, dates, artists, along with docent-like information about each painting.

"Sondra, meet my brother, Stefano."

I don't know what to expect. What kind of female would be the first to capture my driven brother's heart. I guess I painted her in my mind as Corey's twin—a tall, feisty redhead who doesn't take shit from anyone but secretly loves a strong man.

When a cute blonde emerges from the director's office, I realize I was way off. Oh sure, I see the resemblance. They both have the vivid blue eyes. But that's where the similarity ends.

Corey's the type who could pull off a Catwoman in black patent leather. Or wield a crop across some trembling businessman's ass while he licks her thigh-high leather boots.

Sondra's the girl next door. Petite, soft, blonde. She has dimples, for Gods' sake! She's youthful and sweet—probably submissive down to her gentle core.

Nico circles her waist with his arm and kisses her temple. It unnerves me to see my prickly brother so affectionate with someone but in a good way.

I reach for her hand and bring it to my lips.

"Don't."

I stop with her hand midway to my mouth. There's enough danger in my brother's voice for me to know he's serious.

So. He's the jealous kind. Who knew?

I drop it and give Sondra a bow instead. *"Piacere di conoscerti."*

Her glance at Nico confirms my suspicion—definitely submissive. Their relationship is so fucking sweet it warms my heart.

"He said *nice to meet you*. He's a goddamn show-off."

"What?" I shrug. "I just came from the old country."

Nico rolls his eyes.

"Well, I won't intrude anymore. I just wanted to meet the woman who stole my brother's heart."

Sondra blushes, her gaze darting to Nico.

Unbelievable. The girl doesn't know how lost my brother is to her. Well, maybe he wants it that way: like it's a bit of a power or control thing. Nico is definitely as alpha as they come. Or maybe he's just been too busy and now that I'm here, he can show her.

"I'll see you both around. Or maybe I won't. I think I'm supposed to be here so you can spend more time together." I waggle my brows and Nico shakes his head.

"Get out."

"Leaving," I call over my shoulder as I walk to the elevator, a grin tugging at my lips.

CHAPTER 9

orey

I END up going into work an hour early. Call me crazy, it's like the Bellissimo is my addiction. Even after a weekend bender, I can't stay away.

It has nothing to do with not being able to stay away from Stefano Tacone. Nothing at all.

My stomach's still in a tornado over my dad's visit. What if Stefano finds out? Should I confess it outright, the way I did about his job?

But no, then it really will seem like I'm a rat. I mean, I swore to him I have no contact with my dad and then suddenly he's visiting me the minute I get home? It won't look good for me. Like swimming with the fishes bad.

I walk in through the parking garage entrance and stow my purse in my locker.

"You're early," the floor manager, Mac, says.

"Yeah, I can start now, if you want. Otherwise, I'm going to hit the Starbucks before my shift."

"You'll do neither. Mr. Tacone said he wanted to see you in his office the minute you got in."

My heart starts thudding hard. "Which Mr. Tacone?"

"Stefano. The new one." Mac narrows his eyes at me. "Didn't he pull you from the floor Saturday to deal a private game or something?"

My hands are clammy. "Uh, yeah." I look past Mac, wanting to make my escape.

"Well what was it like?" he demands.

Really? This is what we're doing now? Shooting the shit about private games? We aren't even friends.

"It was fine. Kinda stuffy. I prefer the floor, if I had a choice."

"Not sure you do. Whatever Mr. Tacone wants, right?" Now I think he's leering at me, like he's suggesting I slept with Stefano to get into the private games. If he only knew all the kinked-out crazy shit I did with Stefano, he'd have his chin on the floor right now.

"Yeah, well, I'd better get to his office, then," I say, side-stepping around the guy and heading for the security offices.

My heart speeds up even faster as I walk, but I hold my head high. Whatever's waiting for me there, I'll face it. Maybe I can even talk my way out of it.

Or maybe he'll take me as prisoner again. I wouldn't even put up a fuss.

But no. I saw the cool precision with which Stefano Tacone drew a gun and fired at a guy, hitting him square between the eyes. He's not going to fuck around if he thinks I'm a real problem.

I tap on his office door and open it a crack.

Stefano turns from where he's leaning on his desk, talking down to one of the managers. There's no wink. No smile. Just a hard look and a sharp beckon with his hand. "That's it, Joe. Get back out there."

Joe gets up and leaves. I enter.

Stefano locks the door. When he turns and stalks purposefully toward me, I have to work hard not to flinch.

Even when he snatches me up by the waist, I still can't tell the difference between passion and violence.

But then it's clear.

His lips are at my neck, breath hot against my skin. He deposits me at the edge of his desk and pushes me over it. "You're so fucking lucky you came to work early." His hands roam up and down my hips, sliding the fabric of my black mini-skirt up to my waist.

Shivers spread over my skin. "Oh yeah, why's that?"

He gives my ass a slap, then rubs away the sting as his other hand cups my mons. He slaps and soothes again, this time on my other cheek. I imagine the twin hand-prints he left and my pussy clenches. "Because if I had to watch you in this skirt all night without emptying my balls, the fucking you'd get at the end of the night would leave you incoherent." He rubs his fingers over the damp gusset of my panties.

I squirm into his hand. The sex we had this morning feels like so long ago. Or it could be all the tension of seeing my dad and then thinking I was in deep shit with the Tacones is morphing into sexual energy. It doesn't matter what it is, it's caught fire and is pooling in my core, peaking up my nipples.

He tucks his fingers under the gusset of my panties and strokes over my slick.

"What is this, Tacone?" I manage to pant. If I were smart, I wouldn't let this happen. I think I half-expected we'd both pretend nothing happened.

He's my boss. I like my job. This is a disaster waiting to happen.

He pinches my clit. "This is me bending you over my desk for a hard fuck." He sinks a finger into my wetness. "Any objection?" A second finger.

I buck against his skilled touch. Yeah, refusing this isn't an option. Not because I'm feeling coerced. Because I need everything he's about to give to me. "No," I choke.

"Good." He works me over with his fingers, plunging them in me, rubbing my clit, slapping my ass. He keeps it up until I'm up on my tiptoes, thighs trembling with desire.

Then he drags my panties down to my thighs and unbuckles his belt.

For one brief moment, the fantasy of him whipping me with it flashes through my mind. I never thought I'd be into anything like that, but Stefano Tacone does it just right. My ass is still sore from the caning he gave me last night, and I still want him to spank me more.

But he's not interested in punishing me tonight. He rolls a condom on and presses the head of his cock between my petals, parting me.

My teeth sink into my lower lip to stifle a moan.

He eases in slowly, filling me, inch by inch.

I hollow my lower back, encouraging him to sink in deeper.

He tortures me by reversing direction, nearly coming all the way out before he pushes in, a little farther this time.

All I want is for him to spank me and use me roughly. Like a cheap Vegas whore who isn't worth anything more than her perfect Vegas body.

And I never let myself get used.

Ever.

But Stefano was right. Being tied up set me free. And now he doesn't even need duct tape or zip-ties for me to soar. My body responds to his commanding touch. I let him bend me over and tap my ass because it feels dirty and wrong and perfectly right at the same time.

He slams in harder and my hip bones grind against the hard wood of the desk. I brace my hands on the edge of the desk, try to hold my hips away. Stefano must see my dilemma because he slides his arm around the front of my hips and uses it to cushion my pelvis.

The position puts him closer, makes this thing less demeaning. More intimate.

I can't decide if I like the change, but then he's pushing up into me with short, hard thrusts. My breasts bounce with each tormenting stroke, breath strangles.

"Ask me for permission to come."

"You ask me," I counter, just to be contrary. Just because I've already given way too much of myself up in this exchange.

He pinches one of my nipples and twists, making me

gasp. One finger of his other hand settles over my clit and he rubs roughly. "If you come without asking, you're going to be dealing tonight with a hot, throbbing ass."

And that almost makes me come. "May I?" I blurt out because I seriously don't think I can hold it back.

"Come, *bella*. Come all over the cock that owns you."

And that was why I didn't want to beg. I really shouldn't let this man talk to me this way. But I'm already coming, my pussy squeezing and releasing his cock, milking it.

"You're an asshole, Stefano Tacone. How do you say *asshole* in Italian?"

"Still your boss, *bella*." He grips my hips and slams into me, slapping my ass with his loins, making his belt rattle in his dropped pants. He fucks me like a champion until he, too, finds his peak and crests it. Then he slams deep and stays there.

"*Stronzo*."

"What?"

"*Stronzo* is asshole in Italian. But I'm not giving you permission to call me that." He pulls out and tosses his condom into the wastepaper basket. I shudder, thinking every employee who comes in here tonight is going to see it.

He tucks his dick away and buckles his pants, then replaces my panties and skirt. I turn around and he picks me up by the waist and sits me on the desk. "You got a problem we need to talk about?"

I flush. No, other than that I'm shaky and vulnerable from the demeaning sex and I want to be held. But that's not going to happen because Stefano isn't my boyfriend, he's my boss. And we weren't making love, we were fucking. Over his desk. Right before my shift. So I need to pull my shit together and waltz out there in my stilettos to deal some cards.

He brushes my hair back from my face and cups one cheek, studying me.

My face heats some more.

"I am an asshole. For sure. But I mean no disrespect. I really don't."

I believe him. Maybe I was feeling disrespected for a minute there, but it was my own shit. My own fantasy of being used by him became a fear as well.

Still, I need to get the hell out of this office.

"I missed you today, that's all." He strokes my cheek with his thumb.

Goosebumps raise on my skin. He had to go and say *that*?

Someone knocks at the door and I try to hop off the desk, but Stefano won't let me. "Not now," he calls out sharply.

He pulls a keycard out of his pants pocket and tucks it in the inner pocket of my cropped dealer's jacket. "I would love to find you in my bed when I go to my suite tonight." He catches my surprised glance and holds it. His dark brown eyes are warm pools I want to dip into.

"You're giving me the key to your suite?" It strikes me as pretty trusting, although there's probably nothing to steal except for his thousand dollar suits.

"I promise handsome rewards."

"Handsome, huh? Does that mean you?" He flashes his movie-star worthy grin. "Only if you want it to."

So I do have a choice this time. No coercion, just an offer.

And it's one I just might have to accept.

~

Stefano

IT MIGHT BE time to admit I'm obsessed.

Corey Simonson got under my skin in a big, bad way. I watch her all night—the deft movements of her hands with the cards and chips, her confident handling of the bettors. She charms them all: men, women, old, young. They pick her table because she's beautiful and they stay because she's magnetic.

And I want that magnet turned my way.

Forever.

I gave it about a forty percent chance Corey would be in my suite when I went to bed at 3:00 a.m. Usually when I want something I go after it, all guns blazing. But now is not the time to pressure Corey Simonson. Now is the time to give her some space, let her choose on her own. I know she's attracted to me. I know she likes the sex. But she doesn't like being pushed around. And I've already treated her to plenty of that.

Still, it nearly killed me not to seal the deal when her shift was over. I didn't even follow her, or send someone else to follow her. I just let it ride.

The minute I come into my suite, I know she's there. I don't know how—her scent? Or just her energy? It doesn't matter. I know. My nostrils flare with satisfaction. I kick off my shoes and tread softly into the bedroom. She's curled up on her side, her hair falling back from her face and pooling on the pillow behind her.

I tug the sheet down, gently.

She's naked. *Grazie Dio.* I love this woman. She was fucking made for me.

I shuck my clothes and climb in beside her. My dick is hard but I'm not going to wake her. It's enough to know she's here. She *chose* to be here this time.

That's all that matters.

I fit my body around the back of hers and drape an arm over her waist, resisting the urge to cup her breast. If I go there, all bets are off. I'm going to be pinning her to her belly and thrusting until the sun rises.

She mumbles something that ends with my name.

I fucking love hearing her say it in her sleep.

"What's that, *bella?*"

"I'm sleeping with the boss," she mutters on a laugh. "Big mistake, isn't it?"

My chest tightens. "Is it, doll?" I nibble her ear. "I thought you liked veering off the main road."

Her eyelids flutter and lips tug into a smile. "Mmm." She falls back asleep, but I'm glorying in the smile.

Because I know I said the right thing. I might be the wrong guy—a Tacone. Trouble. But she didn't want ordinary. She prefers exciting.

I can be all that, and more for her. All that and more.

CHAPTER 10

tefano

I STAND out on the floor, scanning it for Corey. She's not late, but I'm impatient. I texted her and told her she wouldn't be out on the floor tonight and to wear a dress. She didn't respond. I probably should've given her a little more. She's thinking I'm going to make her deal another private game, I'm sure. But my big plans for her tonight don't involve her dealing or staying at the Bellissimo.

And then I see her. *Madonna*, every time the woman enters a room the heads turn and whatever's playing on the sound system becomes her own personal soundtrack. Right now it's some old Pat Benatar song and someone needs to grab a fan to run ahead and blow Corey's hair back. Strike that, her hair's moving on its own, bouncing and brushing her inviting tits.

131

It's been two weeks of mad sex. I let Corey set the pace, still making it clear I want a piece of her every chance I get. I find her in my bed at least three nights out of the week and I always make sure to reward her for it.

Multiple, blinding orgasms are just the beginning. I treat her to room service and book her appointments at the spa or salon. She's had mani/pedis, facials, massages, reflexology. I bought her a gold thumb ring and diamond studs for the second piercing in her ears.

Tonight she's in a sapphire blue dress, clingy around the hips with a deep V neckline.

I make a beeline for her and catch her hand. She darts a glance around.

"I don't give a fuck who sees us," I snarl. I'm on edge because it's been thirty-six hours since I've been inside her. Plus, I'm nerved up about my plans for the night. They may flop. And it's not like me to ever worry about a date with a girl, but hey, this woman's different.

"You may not, but I *work* here," she complains.

"Like they don't already know." I lead her to the jewelry shop in the casino because her neck looks bare.

"What are we doing?" She fingers the diamond earrings I bought her.

I saunter over to the case as the manager hustles over with a simpering smile. "That one." I point to a blue opal necklace set in white gold. It's a series of three descending pieces, the largest on top.

The manager takes it out and gives it to me. I put it around Corey's neck and hand her the mirror. "What do you think?"

She touches it dubiously. It's hard to know if she

doesn't like it, or doesn't want to accept the gift. There's always a slightly suspicious air from her for anything I do, like I'm tricking her into something.

Maybe I am.

Her eyes slide to the glass cases. Okay. Not the right necklace. I take it off her, scanning the merchandise. Corey doesn't seem interested in anything. Maybe jewelry's not her thing. It's not going to stop me from trying to spoil her, though. I catch sight of an unusual piece in the corner. It's a collar. Not really, but thinking of it that way makes me sprout a chub. It's actually a beautiful piece with moonstones strung in a delicate daisy chain. But it's short. Slave collar short. And the tiny white gold chain hangs down in back like a leash. I point to it and the manager scrambles to get it out.

"This is the one," I say as I put it around Corey's neck. She doesn't even get a say. I want her to wear my collar tonight, and she's going to wear it.

She fingers one of the moonstones. "It's beautiful."

I kiss the place where shoulder meets neck. "You're beautiful. Come on, we have plans."

"Do you want me to box that up for you, Mr. Tacone?" the manager asks. Sue, according to her name tag.

I shake my head. "No, thanks, she'll wear it out." I guide Corey out of the shop and direct her toward the elevators.

"Is it another game?" Corey's voice is tight, and it hits me like a two by four that she's wound up. She has PTSD from the last game.

I stop and spin her to face me. "Baby, what happened last time? That's never going to happen again. That was a one in a thousand chance—a problem I didn't see coming. I'm sorry you had to see it. I'm sorry I put you in danger."

She sucks on her cheek. She might believe me intellectually, but she's still keyed up.

"There's no private game tonight. Not here, anyway. And you're not dealing."

Surprise flickers over her face. "What are we doing, then?"

I wink and incline my head toward the elevators. "It's a surprise. Come on, *amore*. I'm not going to last long with you in that dress wearing my collar."

She allows me to lead her to the elevator and doesn't say another word until we reach the parking garage. Then she touches the necklace. "I knew that's why you picked this one."

I tug the chain in back. "Of course you did."

Corey

STEFANO LEADS me to a black Mercedes and he drives to the Venetian. I shoot him a quizzical look as we get out of the car at the valet station, but he just smiles and escorts me in.

I'm still confused as hell when he takes me to the poker room, takes out a grand in chips and sits down at a no hold em table.

"What are we doing?" I lean over and whisper.

"I'm testing your poker skills," he murmurs back, nodding to the dealer.

"Oh." I sit up taller. I'm suddenly intrigued, challenged and revved up. This isn't some scary mafia deal he's pulling me into. He wants to see me play.

I'm not sure why that's a turn-on, but it is. His interest in me is always a panty-soaker, but knowing it goes beyond my good looks and extends to my brains, my skill, sparks more than just my libido. It lights up my tattered soul.

Stefano orders himself a whiskey, and I get tonic water with lime. I need to stay sharp. Stefano's a decent player, but he seems more interested in observing me. After a couple hands, he gives up his seat and stands over my shoulder.

It takes me a little while to settle into it. I lose fifty bucks (of Stefano's money, so who cares?) on the first three games. Then I stop trying so hard and just go with my first instinct on everything.

Turns out I'm the gut gambler. Who knew? I thought I would've been the cerebral guy.

Five games later, I'm up three hundred.

"Come on," Stefano touches my elbow. "Let's get you into a bigger game." He leads me to a hundred dollar minimum table where I promptly win the next two hands.

Now I feel the energy around me, the way I usually see it with the gut gamblers. It comes in waves: from the people around me, from the cards, from my opponents, from the dealer. I swear I even sense it coming up from the floor, from the cards, and especially, from Stefano. His waves are constant. The others, they have dips and valleys. That's how I know when to bet. When to hold. The energy goes flat for me, I fold. It gets juicy, I bet high. And it works. Every. Fucking. Time.

The dealer pushes stacks of chips my way. I'm up three thousand dollars. I get the nudge to cash it in. I glance at Stefano. "Should we go?"

He nods and I push the chips to the dealer to change them for higher denomination. She pushes six $500 chips my way.

"This is dangerous, Tacone," I say as we walk toward the money-changing station. I slip the chips in his suit pocket. He bankrolled me, after all, and I'm on the clock for him. I figure he keeps my earnings. Besides, he just dropped almost a grand on my necklace—which I absolutely love.

"How so, *bella?*"

"I like it way too damn much."

"Kind of like me?"

I can't stop the smile tugging at my lips. *"Just* like you —a bad bet."

"Mmm." He gets in the line to cash out, clinking the chips together in his pocket.

Once again, I have the sneaking suspicion I offended him. Stefano may be the bad boy, but he doesn't embrace it.

He cashes out and tucks the wad of rolled up hundreds in my purse.

"Thank you." I steal a glance at him from under my lashes as he leads me out. I haven't said thank you much to him. I've been a bitch, really. We got off on the wrong foot and now pushing against him has become a habit.

"Don't thank me. You won it."

I touch his arm as we stand at the valet curb waiting for the car. "I mean thank you for everything. For bringing me here. Showing me what's possible."

"Don't go quitting on me to join the world-wide poker circuit." He winks.

I smile back. "Not quitting. But I totally want to join the circuit."

Stefano opens the passenger door of the Mercedes as it pulls up to the curb. "I can make that happen."

My heart flip-flops in my chest. When he comes around to the driver side and gets in, I have to ask, "Stefano?"

He slides his warm brown gaze over to me as he pulls out. "Yeah, baby?"

"What are we doing?"

At first I think he's not going to understand the question, but then I see a muscle tick in his jaw. He guns the car, zooming into the clogged traffic on the strip, the neon lights casting pink and blue hues across the tinted windows of the luxury vehicle.

"I don't know." His voice is tight—so different from his usual smoky notes.

Hearing that admission—because it sounds so much like truth—actually relaxes me. Stefano isn't playing some game. He doesn't have an ulterior motive.

He's as lost to these forces as I am.

To the lust. The attraction. The magnetic pull to stick together, see how this thing turns out.

His hands grip the steering wheel too tight. It's out of character for the suave, smooth-talking man I first met.

He doesn't speak the rest of the ride back, but when he pulls into the Bellissimo's private parking area and turns off the car, he turns to look at me.

"I want you, Corey, all the fucking time. I need to be in you on a daily basis, but it's not just that. I could sit and just *watch* you for hours. Hell, I just did! I want to know everything that goes on inside that beautiful head. So what is that?"

My breath comes in shallow pants, I can't seem to close my lips. No one—*no one's* ever said anything like that to me before. It's not sugary, not romantic. It's raw and plain and honest. My eyes sting for a moment until I recover. Stefano gets out of the car and slams the door. I can't seem to move until he comes around to open mine and offer his hand. I climb out of the car.

"I don't know. You try to define this; it's not going to fit right. I'm not the one who's gonna give you the white picket fence. I'm the guy who wants to pull your hair and slap your ass and spoil you rotten."

It's almost too much to look into Stefano's face. The intensity there rocks me.

"But you don't want normal, right?" There's something fierce and compelling in Stefano's voice.

I fall into him. I hate my weakness, but being in the circle of his arms makes me strong again. Eases the tremors of uncertainty. He kisses my hair, his hand banding around the back of my neck and holding me.

"I want to take you upstairs and spank your ass red... fuck you until you scream. Then tie you up and do it all over again."

"Well?" I lift my face to his. We're nose to nose, so

close I'm inhaling his whiskey breath. "What are you waiting for?" I whisper hoarsely.

Stefano

I'M itchy as hell to get my dick into Corey but my goddamn phone rings and it's Leo.

"What's up?" I take Corey's hand and hustle her toward the elevator. Inside, I push her up against a wall and press my body against hers, leaning in to nuzzle her neck.

"Feds are here. They want to question you and Corey Simonson."

Fanculo. "Where are they?"

"Nico's office."

"We'll be up in a minute." I hang up. Corey's eyes are the size of saucers. "You heard?"

She nods.

"Everything the way it happened. Donahue lost, he left after Smith, we haven't seen him since. *Capiche?*"

She arranges her face quickly and nods, already appearing composed.

"You sure?"

"I've got it," she says, staring straight ahead.

I curse under my breath. "I'm sorry you have to do this, Corey."

A muscle in her cheek jumps. "Yeah, me too."

The gap between us widens, then, like a goddamn

crack in the earth. She's on one bank, I'm on the other. We're talking to the feds. People she gets. She relates to. *Is* related to. And I'm the criminal. She could fuck me over with one word here. I know she won't. Still, we're on separate teams. I'm asking her to betray her team. She'll do it for me, because… I don't know. I'd like to say she loves me, but I'm not sure that's true. We have a bond, though, I'm sure of that.

We head into Nico's office. We're not touching anymore: no hand holding, no standing close. The physical space between us is nothing compared to the psychic space.

Corey's eyes are alert, attentive. She takes in the agents, shakes their hands. I think I see relief register after she meets them, but that doesn't make sense. She doesn't know these guys.

They take her into a room and question her. It doesn't take long: ten minutes, tops.

When she comes out, it's my turn.

I go in and sit down across from the two yahoos.

"Mr. Tacone, we're investigating the disappearance of Eric Donahue. The last place he was seen was this hotel on the night of the 23rd. Do you recall seeing Mr. Donahue?"

I nod. "Yes. I met him as he was leaving. Kind of a douche."

Agent Spinelli raises his brows. "Oh yeah? How so?"

I shrug. "He thought my brother would be here playing with him. He wasn't thrilled it was just me and I only came in at the end. But what can you do?"

"So Mr. Donahue cashed out and left after you stopped

in. And then what? Did you have any further contact with him?"

"None."

"Did your brother?"

"Not that I know of. Did you ask him?"

They ignore my question. "Did you know Donahue prior to meeting him on the night of the 23rd?"

I shake my head. "Never met him, nor had I heard of him, other than to see he was on the list for the private game."

"Anything else you can tell us about Donahue? His demeanor, anything he mentioned?"

"No. Average guy. Not a great player. He lost, but I wouldn't say he's the suicide type. But I guess you never know." I shrug.

"All right, that's all, Mr. Tacone. Thank you."

I leave the room. Corey's not in the offices, nor is she in the hallway. I head up to my room, but I already know she won't be there.

This investigation draws a line in the sand.

She's on one side of it, and I'm on the other.

Corey

I DRIVE home after the questions from the feds because I'm too shaken up to stay. The hot sex with Stefano would've been tepid, at best.

Why were they questioning us at eleven at night

anyway? Oh, maybe because that's when the staff who worked the night the guy went missing are in the casino?

My dad wasn't one of the feds asking questions, which was a huge relief. I seriously couldn't have handled him in the same building as Stefano. I think I could combust. But his absence is curious. Does it mean he's working undercover on this?

Or is it not his case and he just volunteered to question me because he knows I work here? Or more likely, because he heard about Sondra's engagement?

What a dick.

My phone buzzes while I'm unlocking my front door. It's a text from Stefano.

Stefano: *Grrr*

I standing just inside my door and stare at the screen, guilt splashing through me. We'd had an awesome date. I totally left him blue-balled.

I start to text *sorry*, but change my mind and hit the call button instead.

"Corey." He sounds relieved I called.

"I'm sorry I ran out. I just... was unnerved and needed to regroup." I drop my purse and keys on the table and kick off my heels.

"Yeah, I get it. I'm sorry you had to do that for me."

For me. Our relationship has shifted enough that all pretense of threats are gone. He knows things are personal now. I am doing it for him. For sure.

"Rain check?" I fill a glass with ice water in my kitchen.

"Of course. Tomorrow night?"

He's asking me. For once, Stefano Tacone is asking,

not telling. It's nice, not that I mind the telling, either. It suits him to play bossman and he does it so well.

"I should probably get some shifts in so I can pay my rent."

"You're still on payroll, baby. And you just made three grand tonight."

"Oh yeah," I laugh. I had actually forgotten because the money didn't seem real to me.

"Next week I'll get you in a high stakes game. See if you can win big."

Judging by the way my heart picks up speed and my whole body turns on, I'd say I want this. How Stefano knows, I have no idea. Or maybe I'm just excited *because* he's a part of it.

"You really think I can do this?"

"I do," he says without hesitation. "But it's not about whether you win or lose. That's not why I'm entering you."

"Why, then?"

"I think you'll enjoy it. Stretch yourself a bit. Use your talents in a new way. I think it could be fun."

My chest has gone gooey and warm. Since when did Stefano Tacone care about my fun? About my sense of fulfillment?

I experience a stab of guilt and not giving him the same kind of thought. All I've been doing is keeping him at arm's length. Barricading my heart from the sexy playboy of the Bellissimo.

But he's not acting like a player.

He's acting like a boyfriend.

Now I wish I'd stayed the night at the Bellissimo.

"Thank you. It… it means a lot to me what you're doing."

I hear Stefano's exhale through the line. "Tomorrow night, *amore*. You can show me your appreciation."

My laugh sounds husky. I lie on my bed and bring my hand between my legs. "I can do that."

"And expect punishment. You don't leave me blue-balled without paying penance, *bella*."

My pussy clenches. "I'm sure you'll make it a good lesson," I purr.

Stefano curses softly in Italian. "You kill me, you know that?"

"It's mutual," I murmur. "See you tomorrow." I end the call and fall back on my pillow, working my fingers between my legs as I picture my sexy as hell lover.

It's definitely mutual, Stefano.

orey

"Why don't you just move in here?" Stefano asks me a few weeks later. We've been seeing each other most every day, either at work or when he takes me off the schedule and brings me out on the town with him instead. Thanks to his continued interest in showing me what's possible, I won ten thousand dollars last week playing poker.

This morning, I'm leaving his suite to go home for the day and he's grumpy about it. I spend the night in his suite three or four nights a week, but he's starting to put the pressure on.

"What's in your shitty little apartment that you don't have here?"

"Don't be a dick," I mutter, hopping to put on my high heels from last night.

"No really." He knots his tie, completing the male model look and nearly drawing a sigh from me. "What is it? I want to know."

"Well, a fully stocked kitchen for one."

His face clears. "You like to cook?" He looks so happy, I almost blush.

"Yeah. I like to know exactly what I'm putting in my mouth."

He smirks. "Ah. I get it. You need to control what you eat."

I pick up one of his balled up socks from the floor and throw it at his head.

"I'm right, aren't I?"

"Shut up."

He grins. "So you want a kitchen. We'll kick Leo and Tony out of the top floor and move back into my place up there. Then would you stay?"

I flush some more. I'm still not ready to make that kind of move with Stefano. This is too intense. Too fast. I'm not someone who's quick to trust and I definitely don't give my heart away easy. In fact, I'm not sure I've ever given it up. I probably have my dad to thank for that, too.

Stefano's smile fades. "Pack your shit, you're moving." His voice turned into Demanding Asshole Boss tones.

"You ordering it doesn't make it happen," I snip back.

"*Cuore mio.*" He walks toward me, his voice soft and dangerous, his tread like a panther's. He picks me up by the waist and sits my ass on the desk. "It's going to happen." He pushes my thighs open and brings his thumb to my clit through my jeans. "The less resistance you provide, the greater the reward." He pinches one nipple through my shirt and bra. His teeth graze my shoulder. "You give me trouble? There's going to be punishment. The clock starts now. You have forty-eight hours to get your shit packed and ready. Every hour you delay after that? I'm going to make you pay." He nibbles my earlobe. "Think about it, *amore*." He cups my chin and kisses me, hard. "You need help packing, I'll send some guys over. Just say the word. But this is happening."

I blink up at him. Part of me wants to give in. What's holding me back, anyway? But getting tangled up with Stefano feels way too scary. What happens when things go south? I won't have my own place to live in. I'll be out of a job.

He rubs my clit and tugs my nipple in time together and I spread my knees wider, needing more now. I reach for the bulge in his pants and squeeze.

Stefano works the button of my jeans open and pulls me off the desk to shimmy my jeans and panties down below my butt. He presses a finger inside me, then a second. I squirm as he resumes his torture of my nipple, thrusting his digits at the same time. When he brings his thumb to my clit, I clutch his hand, trying to shove his fingers deeper.

He withdraws them and puts them in his mouth, tasting me.

I wait, panting. I'm sure he's going to fuck me now. Pull his cock out and give it to me rough and hard, like he always does, but instead he gives my pussy a slap. "No orgasm for you, and don't you dare try to give yourself one. This pussy belongs to me."

A spike of white-hot anger zips through me. Yeah, redhead. I glare as I yank my pants up. "Fuck you, Tacone."

"Hey." He catches my arm. I register alarm on his face, regret even, but I don't care. It's probably just the sexual frustration, but I'm pissed. Ready to knee him in the balls again, pissed.

Although I wouldn't do that to him again.

"Hey." He matches my intensity, spinning me around and pinning my arms behind my back. He pushes my torso down over the desk and smacks my ass.

"Stefano," I grit through my teeth.

He smacks me again. "Yes?"

"You'd better fuck me now or I will seriously never speak to you again."

He doesn't answer, but starts spanking me, hard and fast.

It's exactly what I need, the sharp slaps matching my fire, meeting me, channeling my fury into something more sensual. More satisfying.

I struggle, not because I want to get away, but because he's right; I like to be held captive. I like to know I can't escape, to feel his strength, to surrender to his will, which I know will leave me satisfied.

He doesn't stop—not until my ass burns, even with the protection of my jeans. A mixture of triumph and relief rushes through me when he finally releases my arms and works open the button of my jeans, the bulge of his cock pressed insistently against my ass.

Flutters bloom in my belly. Stefano shoves my pants

and panties down a second time, then slaps me between the legs.

I groan. I don't even register the smack as pain. It's all a means to release, to satisfaction. "Please," I mumble. I guess all my bluster is gone. I'm his now—all it took was a spanking. Or the knowing I'll soon get what I need.

I hear the crinkle of foil as Stefano makes sure to protect me, and then he slams in all the way. I gasp at the sensation of being nearly split in two. Stefano shudders, staying buried in me. Whether it's for me to adjust or for him, I can't be sure. One thing I do know—when he starts, he's going to bring it.

He grips my hips and, as expected, backs up and slams in hard again. The rhythm he sets is fast and brutal. My hands fly to the desk to brace myself, lift my face off the desk before I get hurt.

I sink into the experience, surrender completely lost in the waves of sensation that cascade through me. The phone flies off the desk. A notepad, my phone charger. I both need to come and don't want it to end.

Stefano changes to quick up-thrusts, changing the angle to fill me even more.

I moan and whine, push my torso up so I'm leaning on my hands. I look over my shoulder at him, already sorry for my temper. Wanting to make sure he's not mad.

He is. His jaw flexes, eyes are black and unforgiving. He catches my hair in his fist and pulls my mouth back to his, dragging his lips across mine. I kiss him back, eager to give now, wanting to speed his satisfaction so I get mine.

Need.

Must.

Please.

"Stefano," I pant when he breaks the kiss.

"Tell me you're moving in." His guttural tones are hard, more a growl than words. His loins slam into my smarting ass with thrust after forceful thrust.

"Okay!" I surrender. "Yes, I'll move in."

"*Now,*" he demands. He's totally pissed.

"Now, yes."

Tears spike my eyes for a reason I can't fully comprehend, but Stefano comes and he pinches my clit and a nipple at the same time so I come, too. I toss my head back on a strangled cry, my body bucking against his, pussy milking his cock for all it's worth.

Stefano gentles, stroking a hand up and down my throat while still buried inside me. He kisses the side of my face and I turn away.

"I'm keeping my apartment," I say, like I'm a child who has to win one small point.

Stefano pulls out and throws away the condom while I pull my pants back up and zip them. When he returns, he spins me around and cradles my head. He kisses me once, sensually, his lips gliding over mine.

"Okay. I get it. You need to know you have somewhere to go if this doesn't pan out." He watches my face closely and must see confirmation there, because he nods. "Fine. You do what you need to do. But if you think I don't want to burn that fucking place to the ground, you're delusional."

My lip curls. "Why?" I demand.

"You lived there with your *testa di cazzo* ex. I don't like you being there."

I admit I'm surprised. Stefano hasn't shown jealousy before. I figure he's confident enough, he doesn't have to worry. Maybe I read it wrong.

"It was my place before he lived there. I paid the rent. I cleaned. He was just an asshole who lived there for a while."

"Okay." Stefano still doesn't sound happy, but he's conceding. He strokes my cheek with his thumb. "Are you okay?"

I give a wry smile. "Do you mean is my ass okay?"

"No, I mean us. Are we good?"

"Because you just railroaded me into what you want?"

He winces.

I inch closer to him, even though we're standing toe to toe. "I don't know. I feel a bit raw."

He immediately wraps his arms around me and pulls me against his chest. "Yeah, me too," he whispers against my hair.

I lean into his strength, wondering how I became the biggest coward on the face of the Earth. Why do I have so many barriers up? What am I afraid of losing—my heart? My pride? Are they so damn important?

"You want me to help you pack?"

"Like you personally? Or you'll send someone over?"

"Me personally. Me and you—packing your shit together."

It sounds great, actually. A pain in the ass, but great. "Yeah, I'd like that."

He releases me from the hug to stroke my hair back from my face. "Okay. Let's go."

~

Stefano

I'M cheerful as hell packing Corey's shit that afternoon. Yeah, I was an asshole about it and I feel bad, but I won. She's giving something more of herself to me.

And yeah, I still know our relationship is complicated as hell considering who our fathers are, but I don't want to worry about that now. All I care about is getting closer to Corey. Getting into her head. Having her near me at all times.

At four o'clock I get a text from Junior, my oldest brother.

Che due coglioni! I groan when I read it.

Corey twists from where she's standing. "What is it?"

"My fucking brother."

"What did Nico say?"

I growl and stuff my fingers through my hair. "Not Nico. Junior—the oldest *stronzo*. He says he's bringing all the guys to Vegas this weekend for Nico's bachelor party."

Corey straightens. "I didn't know Nico was having a bachelor party this weekend."

"Yeah, he wasn't," I grumble.

Fucking Junior.

"Ah. It's a surprise ambush."

I flick a glance at her, surprised she gets it. "Exactly. And I'm supposed to set everything up."

"This is the brother who tried to kill Nico when they were in Chicago?"

"Not tried," I correct. Junior doesn't try. He doesn't fail. He gets done whatever the hell he wants to get done, just like our father. "Threatened."

"I'm sorry," she says simply. "Family sucks."

"Understatement." My family lives and breathes by *La Famiglia*. Blood is important. Only family can be trusted.

Supposedly.

And it was family money that funded the Bellissimo, helped Nico generate millions. But when you're afraid for your life just because you want to marry the woman of your own choosing?

That's just plain fucked up.

So Junior bringing everyone out for a bachelor party isn't to help celebrate with Nico. It's using him at best. They'll turn the wedding into every form of business tactic they need it to be. PR for the family, greasing wheels, a deadline for people who owe them money.

Nico will be expected to perform like a trained monkey. Act the jovial host to everyone, make a stand when needed. He'll take it fine. He'll do his part. And so will I, of course.

Because really—what other choice do we have?

CHAPTER 12

 orey

I STAND in one of my red dresses, shuffling cards, waiting for the party to start. We're in one of the conference rooms on the third floor, but it's been set up as a private lounge tonight, with couches and tables. A buffet table of party food is set up against one wall and a bartender stands at attention behind a bar.

Nico called me last night, after Stefano and I finished moving all my clothes and personal items into one of the penthouse suites.

"I need you to do something for me," he said, without any preamble. Stefano was out on the floor, working and I was still unpacking and arranging things. Nico hadn't called me before, except when Sondra broke up with him and went home to Michigan. Then he rode my ass non-stop trying to get me to tell him where she was.

"Okay. What is it?"

"I need you to deal for a private gig tomorrow night. A bachelor party."

"*Your* bachelor party?"

"Yes." He sounded exasperated, but I didn't think with me.

"Well, you're the boss. Tell me when and where and I'll be there."

"I'll text you the details. I haven't told Stefano yet, but I need you to be there."

I try to read between the lines. Why does he need *me*? *Oh.* That's freaking sweet.

"To put Sondra's mind at ease?" I asked.

"Right. It won't be pretty: strippers and prostitutes and cigars. I don't want her worrying. *Capiche*?"

"No problem. I will be her eyes and ears. She can count on me."

"Atta girl. Now just don't let Stefano change your orders. I need you there, I don't give a shit if he objects."

He hung up before I could question why Stefano would object. It better not be because he wanted to party with strippers.

An uneasy sensation twisted through my belly because I could picture it all too easily. Stefano with an arm around a bimbo on each side. Stefano getting his dick sucked by one while he slapped the other's ass.

But no. He was anything but excited about this bachelor party. And a man with his looks and personality wouldn't ever have to pay for sex.

Nico was right, though. Stefano was pissed when he found out I'm dealing for tonight. Even now, as he walks briskly around, barking orders and getting things settled, I can see he's uptight. He comes off as angry with me, but I'm trying not to take it personally.

I know how it is with family.

I'm never Miss Sunshine around my dad. Or my mom for that matter, even though I love her. Maybe I resent her for being a doormat to my dad—for marrying him in the first place. I don't know what it is, but she drives me freaking bonkers, too.

The door bursts open and Nico comes in first, followed by a stream of Italian men—dozens of them. Most look older than Nico and Stefano, but there are some younger guys, too. They've been drinking already. Maybe they started at a bar downstairs.

"Stefano, where are the girls?" a guy about ten years older than Nico demands. He pronounces Stefano's name with an Italian accent, so it's STAY-fano instead of STEH-fano.

"Ten minutes, Junior," Stefano calls back, his affable smile in place, even though I can tell it's fake. He cranks up the music, lowers the lights and flicks his gaze to me. He's been almost curt all evening, and now he scowls.

I give him a *what?* shrug and he shakes his head.

Two hours later, the party is totally out of hand. Topless girls in nothing more than G-strings straddle laps on the sofas and chairs. One of them got fucked right in front of the entire group.

"You put your dick in a girl, you're paying extra,"

Stefano shouted to raucous laughter. "I'm only paying for the strip tease."

Sondra will be relieved to know Nico hasn't even looked at a girl. She's not the jealous type, but she has a history with men who cheat, and then Nico failed to mention he had a marriage contract to another woman when they started dating, so it's a sore spot.

The visitors are all having a grand old time. The guys I recognize from the casino—the ones who live here in Vegas—they're unimpressed by the whole affair. They all appear to be working tonight rather than enjoying the event.

Nico's big bodyguard, Tony, stands at attention at the door, stepping up to interfere every time a guy gets too rough or handsy with a girl. I notice nobody gives him any shit back. Of course, he is monster huge. Considering how protective he is of the women, I'm guessing he's actually a big softy. I've talked to him a couple times and he seemed like a stand-up guy.

I've been dealing for two hours straight and I'm ready for a break, but I don't think anyone's going to relieve me soon.

The guy at my right gets louder and handsier with each new drink, each passing moment.

"Hit me again, beautiful," he slurs, and palms my ass. His groping is nothing new and I step back out of his reach. This time, though, he gets aggressive and lunges forward to slap my ass. "Don't move away when I'm talking to you."

I'm annoyed but not too worried. All I have to do is get Tony's attention if the problem continues.

Fortunately, Nico appears behind the guy and grabs his shoulder. "Hey, hands off this one; she's not a stripper."

"Aw, come on. She's perfect!" The jackass stands up and comes at me, grabbing both my breasts.

Nico pulls back on the guy's collar, but Stefano arrives like a tornado, jerking the guy back and punching him with a wicked right hook.

I dodge his toppling body and he crashes into my side of the table.

"Whoa, whoa." Nico throws an arm around Stefano's chest and yanks him back. "Take it easy." Stefano's expression is a dark storm. His black gaze is laser-focused on my groper. He is nowhere near finished.

"Stefano!" I snap, hoping to bring him back.

He continues to fight for his freedom.

"Enough!" Nico counsels. "He didn't know she belongs to you. Now he knows. Take a fucking breath."

Belongs to you. That's the way these guys think. Like a woman is a piece of property.

"This is your girl?" the guy sneers, pointing from me to Stefano. "Why in the hell would you have her as entertainment at a fucking bachelor party? She's a whore?"

Stefano goes crazy again and Nico releases him. Stefano decks the guy, knocking him into the table again, then he holds his shirt and punches his jaw again. I swear Nico takes his time before he and Tony pull him off.

"Really, Bobby? That's what you want to say to my brother when he already wants to shove your balls up your ass?" Nico says. He's all calm and in control while Stefano's a raging bull.

The guys all laugh.

159

"Apologize to her." Spit flies from Stefano's mouth.

The guy wipes blood with a stupid grin on his face.

Stefano lunges again. "I said—"

"Yeah, yeah, I heard you. I'm sorry, Miss—"

"Simonson," Nico provides.

"Simonson," Tony repeats it like the idiot should recognize the name. I mean, he should, but clearly he's drunk and probably stupid to begin with, so I don't think he's going to. "She's the bride's fucking cousin, and now you know why she's in here, *coglione*." Tony fills in. "She's spying on Nico. So put your dick away and act like a fucking gentleman."

"Get her out of here," Nico says, finally releasing Stefano.

Fury still knotting his expression, he reaches out a hand.

I take it and allow him to lead me out of the room.

Stefano

I'M TOO PISSED to see straight. That *testa di cazzo* had his fucking paws all over Corey, and I still want to kill him.

And I'm pissed at myself for losing my shit.

I didn't want Corey to see me like this. Ever.

This is a side of myself I'd prefer didn't exist—the Tacone temper. An inheritance from my father's side, or perhaps simply nurtured into me through exposure to violence from a young age.

I've been trying to make Corey believe I'm something else. Something beyond a shady mafioso. Something sophisticated and trustworthy and fucking upstanding.

But Junior had to roll into town with the whole pack of *guidos* and expose me for what I am.

One of them.

Chauvinistic, paternalistic, low-class seedy bastards who grope prostitutes and act like assholes.

"Hey," Corey says softly when we get in the elevator.

I can't even look at her. I'm so goddamn ashamed. Ashamed and angry. I pace around the small elevator, stabbing my fingers through my hair.

"Hey," she repeats, grabbing the lapels of my jacket and stepping into my space. She drops her hand down to cup my balls and suddenly it's on.

Fighting already gives me a cockstand, so it's easy to switch gears from fight to fuck. My dick lurches into her hand and I spin her around and pin her against the elevator wall. The doors ding and open at our floor, but I hit the button for the rooftop, and they close again.

"Get those long fucking legs up around my waist," I growl like she's in deep trouble, when really, I'm the guy who ought to be on his knees right now.

She complies and I thrust into the notch between her legs, the damp heat of her pussy providing the beacon for my aching cock.

The elevator doors open and I carry her out, right onto the roof. The Bellissimo has a rooftop restaurant a few stories below, but this roof is utilitarian, with HVAC, mechanical systems and other equipment. I push her up against the HVAC unit and work my zipper open to free my erection.

I tear her panties off with a tug that makes her squeal and then I'm in her, sinking into her heat.

I'm mindless with need, thrusting like my life depends on it. Like if I just get deep enough, I can erase every hurt and anger I've ever suffered. Like her pussy is home base and if I can just get deeper, just claim it completely, I'll have won.

Corey wraps her arms around my neck, hangs on and rides me, her hips tilted to take me deeper, her little moans and cries the soundtrack to my lust.

"I need you, baby," I mutter, frantic to just fuck her harder, just get deeper.

"I know, I know," she pants.

I lean in and bite her neck, hang on with my teeth, making her whimper on the next thrust.

And then I'm gone.

Heat flashes at the base of my spine, my balls tighten up.

I lose my vision—or maybe I close my eyes, I can't tell —but everything goes black, stars burst from the periphery as I roar loud enough for all of fucking Las Vegas to hear.

Corey screams, too and I come, emptying into her, her pussy milking—

Oh fuck.

I yank out, coming on the wall between her thighs, on her dress, on my hand. Her feet drop abruptly to the ground

"Fuck, baby. I didn't protect you. I'm so sorry. I lost

my head."

"It's fine; we're fine. I got on the pill last week."

I sag in relief. "I'm clean. I swear to you."

"I am, too. I just got checked."

"*Grazie Dio.*" I lean my forehead against hers. For a moment I stay there, just breathing her breath, keeping our connection. "I'm sorry you saw me like that. I'm embarrassed, Corey."

She wraps her arms around the back of my head, burrowing her fingers into my hair. "Are you kidding?" She massages my scalp, gazes up at me with her electric blue eyes. "No one's ever defended me before. I'm not the kind of girl who plays damsel in distress, in fact, part of me wants to tell you off for assuming I couldn't handle it myself. But, Stefano, I'm pretty much swooning right now. You're a knight in fucking shining armor."

I stroke the sides of her waist, trying to contain my anger over her first words—*no one's ever defended her before.* How can that be? Not a parent? A friend? "I guess people usually assume you *can* handle things on your own. Hell, I *know* you can. But that doesn't mean I'm not gonna go in swinging for you every fucking time."

She traces her fingernails down the sides of my neck. "Swoon," she murmurs.

"Yeah, baby, I'll make you swoon." I curl my forearm under her knees and sweep her into the air, damsel style. "Let me take you back to my bed."

She laughs—a husky sound—and kisses my neck.

I carry her to the elevator, and refuse to put her down. Even when we get into our suite, I keep holding her, bringing her to the balcony, where I sit on the wicker loveseat and arrange her on my lap.

I stroke her back, dismayed to discover it's covered in tiny scrapes from the wall of the HVAC.

"No one ever defended you?" I ask. "Even when you were little?"

She sighs. "My mom's a doormat. That's why she married my asshole dad, I guess. Sondra's parents stayed out of it. I think my dad intimidated them, too. Sondra would've stuck up for me, but I'm a year older, so I was always the know-it-all. I didn't let her nurture me much. It was always the other way around."

I kiss her shoulder.

"Who was that guy, anyway? Anyone you need to worry about pissing off?"

I scoff. "No. He's some cousin. Nobody important. That's why Nico let me get a few swings in." Speaking of Nico, I'm an asshole to make him break up shit at his own bachelor's party. I pull out my phone and text an apology.

Corey watches me. "You and Nico are close."

"Yeah. Way closer than we are to our older brothers. Nico was my defender growing up. He protected me. We're different from the rest of them, at least I like to think so. We didn't take to family business, even though it was shoved down our throats. Honestly, I think Nico started hatching the plan for the Bellissimo way back in high school. Trying to scheme his way into a different future. And I'm lucky he took me with him."

"Were you here from the beginning?"

I nod. I still remember breaking ground on this project —Nico and I showing up to supervise the contractors. "I got pulled back into family shit two years ago and had to go to Chicago. Then Sicily."

"And are you back to stay now?" She shifts on my lap to catch my eyes.

Is she asking about our future?

Can we even have one?

"Yeah. If Nico needs help, no one else in the family can pull me away. Nico's profits trump all else, so he can demand the soldiers he requires."

My phone buzzes and I check the message. It's from Nico. *I'm leaving. They're too shit-faced to notice. Tony's staying to keep an eye on things.*

I'm relieved he didn't demand I come back. I should offer, but I don't want to. I just want to hold Corey. Share secrets with her. Break in our new bed.

Corey climbs off my lap. "Do you have to go back down there?"

I stand and wrap my arm around her waist from behind, pull her back against me. "Nope. I'm staying right here with you, *bella*."

"Good," she murmurs. "Let's go to bed."

CHAPTER 13

 orey

"TELL me this isn't a surreal experience for you." I straighten Sondra's wedding gown in the back and pour two glasses of champagne. We're in her bridal suite, waiting for the ceremony to begin.

"Out of body," she confirms. "Why didn't we elope? This is insane." She looks beautiful in an open-back filmy affair, her hair in a loose up-do. The bouquet is champagne pink roses. I'm in a midnight blue cocktail dress, fitted over the hips with a flare at the calf.

Nico and Sondra's wedding is an evening affair, on the top floor of one of Chicago's ritziest hotels. Nico hired a wedding planner who consulted with Sondra, so we're pretty stress-free, other than having to deal with the two sets of families who couldn't be more different.

At least my dad wasn't invited. Sondra's parents leaned on her hard, but she didn't budge. Of course, leaving him off the guest list wasn't just for me. It's for the entire Tacone family who wouldn't appreciate the presence of a fed at any family gathering.

But even without that movie-worthy stressor, mixing Sondra's midwestern family with the Tacone clan is pretty hilarious. If you have a sense of humor. Which we're working on.

I hand her a champagne flute and clink it with mine. "Drink up. It will help. I promise."

She gives a nervous laugh and we both drink. I guess we're making up for her lack of a bachelorette party now. Nico attempted to head off the stereotypical Vegas girls gone wild by sending us to a spa week at the ritzy Miraval resort in Tucson. I have to say it was way better than anything I would've planned.

A knock sounds on the door and I answer it. Stefano's leaning against the doorframe in a perfectly-fitted tux, looking GQ worthy. "Hey, *bella*." He gives me a lazy smile. "Are you ladies ready? The show's about to begin."

I pick up our bouquets and hand Sondra hers. "Ready as we'll ever be." I toddle out on my dyed-to-match stilettos, which seem to be a half-size too small.

We head to the doors for our big entrance. There's an adorable flower girl and two little ring bearers. Sondra said Mrs. Tacone nearly had a meltdown, wanting every member of the family to be in the wedding party, but Nico ran interference. His other three brothers serve as ushers, which, even in their tuxes, makes them look like bouncers or bodyguards.

I'm the maid of honor and Stefano stands as best man, which means he's the guy who walks me down the aisle. I try to ignore the little voice in my ear telling me this could be us. We could be the bride and groom. It feels so easy. So possible.

But it's really not.

The ceremony is blessedly short. My Aunt Susie, Sondra's mom, is wiping tears from the minute Sondra walks down the aisle until they're declared husband and wife.

Afterward, we suffer through the photo shoot and then a sit-down dinner. I position myself in a seat near my mother and Sondra's mom where I can watch everyone. I'm fascinated by the Tacone clan, the boisterous talking and gestures, the dark-haired good looks. Stefano and Nico's mom is still lovely—clearly the source of Stefano's beauty. And they have a younger sister, Alessia who is drop-dead gorgeous.

A full twenty-instrument band sets up and starts playing, and Nico leads Sondra out for the first dance.

Ugh, dancing. The thought of attempting anything but sitting in the damn bridesmaid shoes makes me grit my teeth. Fuck it. I'll go find another pair. Who cares if they don't match perfectly?

I leave for my hotel room. Outside the banquet room, a few people walk through the hallway, mostly hotel staff. But then a familiar figure appears and I stop in my tracks.

My dad smiles. "Hello, Corey."

I'd like to say I remained cool and calm, but considering the chill that sweeps through me, I probably lose all the color in my face.

"What are you doing here? You weren't invited."

"I'm working." Of all the things he might have said, this is the worst. He's still working the murder case. Which means Stefano is still a suspect. Maybe there's even more to it I don't know. All of them could be under investigation: Nico, Leo, Stefano, Tony. Me.

I don't care about me, though. Turns out I care about the Tacones.

A lot.

Whatever they've done—and I have to believe they're not entirely innocent—I don't want any of them to go down. In fact, I would do almost anything to keep that from happening.

"This is a fucking wedding," I snarl. "Unless you have a warrant, you need to leave now." I pull my phone out and let my thumb hover over the screen. "Believe me, I can call some guys who will be happy to throw you out."

He grips my arm, way too hard. "What kind of idiot did I raise?" He's been drinking. I smell it on his breath even though he seems perfectly in control. "You need to get away from these criminals, before they take you down with them—you and your little cousin."

Little cousin. For fuck's sake! I yank my arm away, but it takes some doing. I'll have bruises there tomorrow.

"You know your boyfriend is my prime suspect?"

"*Get out!* I'm calling security." It's a bluff, though. The last thing I want is for the Tacones to know my freaking father is here.

This is my fault. My relationship with Stefano probably prompted his investigation. It's just like my dad to need to ruin my life just to prove I was wrong. He was right.

My head suddenly aches. My stomach feels like I swallowed an anchor.

My dad gives a humorless chuckle. "I'm leaving. If you were smart, you would too."

I watch his back as he walks away. I hate the man.

If the force of my hate was combustible, he'd go up in flames right now.

And I do just want to leave right now. My entire body feels the effects of the meeting; my hands tremble, head pounds.

"There you are," Stefano says, walking toward me, an affable smile on his face. It fades when he sees me. "What's wrong?"

I rub my temples. "Uh, I have a migraine." Not a lie. "I'm going to head to my hotel room to take something and change my shoes. I'll be back in a few, okay?"

He scoops me up into his arms. "Are those shoes bothering you? I'll have to carry you, then."

My laugh is forced. He frowns, looking down at me. "Did something happen?" His voice is suddenly quiet. Almost deadly.

If I weren't already tense, I would've gone stiff. "No, nothing." I hate lying to him. It makes me feel like I'm going to puke. "Hey, will you put me down? It hurts my head even more." Now I feel like a bitch on top of it.

He stops and lowers me to my feet, his brows together.

"Just give me a few minutes. I need to regroup."

He nods and shoves his hands in his pockets, looking

at me thoughtfully. I ignore the chills racing up and down my spine as I walk swiftly to my hotel room.

Get it together, Corey. Get your shit together.

Stefano

SOMETHING HAPPENED TO COREY, I'm sure of it. If one of my asshole family members roughed her up, I will fucking kill them. It's possible Junior found out about her dad. Wouldn't he say something to me first, though? Or to Nico?

Or is it her own family that has her off her game. Lord knows, I can sympathize with that plight.

I knew this wedding would be a fuck-all of family shit. Corey said her dad wasn't invited. Maybe someone gave her a hard time about that.

I wish to hell she would just tell me!

All she ever does is push me away. Enough that I'm not even sure she feels the same way.

Not that I've come out and said I love her, or declared long-term intentions. I still haven't figured my way around her dad and my family. I still don't even know what long-term looks like for me and her. If I even know how to be in a committed relationship.

Hell, just getting her to move in with me was a major endeavor.

She probably won't be walking down that aisle with me as anything but best man for a long time.

If ever.

She's been wounded. Her dad did a number on her and she's gun shy now. But I'm going to show her what it's like to be with someone who has your back. Because if there's anything good I learned from my family, it's loyalty.

It's the willingness to die or go down for the people you love.

And eventually I'll teach her to trust me.

CHAPTER 14

orey

NICO FLEW us all to Chicago in a private plane, but we're on our own heading back because he and Sondra are taking the private plane to Fiji for their honeymoon.

Stefano and I head to the lobby at 7:00 a.m. the next morning to get a taxi to the airport. After the incident with my dad last night, I'd gone to my hotel room to pull myself together, and made it through the rest of the night.

Stefano dragged me back from the shitstorm of thoughts in my head at the end of the night by pinning me down—literally with my wrists clamped in his big paws—and forcing me to hold eye contact the entire time he fucked me raw.

It was brutal. And beautiful. By the time we both came

RENEE ROSE

—perfectly synchronized together, of course—I was fully present. In my body. With him.

We get to the airport, and Stefano hands the tickets over to the United agent. "Two to Memphis," she confirms.

My head jerks up. "No—"

"That's right," Stefano says.

I hide my confusion because I don't want to get punked in front of the ticket agent, but the minute we head for security, I grab his arm and pull him to a stop. "What in the hell is going on?"

He hides a smile. "The world poker tournament starts tonight. I entered you."

My eyes must fill my whole face. "What?"

"You heard me, *bella*, you're going to be on TV. An international poker star."

My knees nearly buckle. "Stefano, are you nuts? It costs ten grand just to get in. I'm nowhere near ready for games like those."

Stefano's expression turns serious. "Bullshit." He has a way of saying *bullshit* that is all street. All scary, in your face, I-dare-you-to-lie-again attitude.

I draw back, flushing.

"When are you going to let yourself out of the box?" he demands.

I'm trembling now, whether it's from anger or fear, I'm not sure. "What box?" I raise my voice, because getting right back in his face is my defense mechanism.

"The box you put yourself in to keep you small. To keep you from shining. Who are you hiding your brilliance from? Your dad? Yourself?"

I slap his chest, because tears are shoving up in my throat and I'm pissed that he's stripping me bare right here in the airport.

He catches my hand and brings it to his lips, kissing it with tenderness. "Because I see it in you every time I look, *bella*," he murmurs. "Every goddamn time. And I want you to know what I know."

Tears well up. "What's that?" I mutter.

"There's nothing you can't do."

"Damn you, Stefano." I blink back the water in my eyes.

"Listen, *amore*. We're going to Memphis. If you decide you don't want to play, then we'll go to Graceland and see the King. Or we'll stay in the hotel room and you can punish me for springing this on you. 'Kay?"

A few tears spill and I let out a watery laugh. "Yeah. Okay. Asshole."

"Still your boss, baby." He gives me a mock-stern look that makes my toes curl.

I let him lead me through the security line and into our first-class seats on the airplane where my eyes start to water again.

My boyfriend.

Sheesh.

No one has ever been this sweet to me in my whole life.

And knowing that makes me even sicker thinking about my dad and his goddamn investigation.

I need to stop him.

And actually, this poker championship may give me the way.

∾

Stefano

TWENTY BUCKS WILL GET you a long way with most any stranger. I have a clutch of them in my hand and I'm offering them up in what may be the craziest thing I've ever attempted.

I must be in love.

That's the only explanation for this scene I've facilitated outside the room of Corey's first poker match. I told her I needed to make a few phone calls and that I'd pick us up some coffee and meet her here.

She wasn't thrilled about being left alone. I think her nerves were getting to her, but she didn't seem suspicious.

Now, though, I'm starting to worry that she won't show. I did tell her she didn't have to if she didn't want.

What if she never comes down?

"How's this look?" A pretty millennial with a makeup pencil in her hand asks. She's written C-O-R-E-Y across her face. A group of her friends are working on the TEAM COREY banner. They're all wearing the Corey sashes I had pre-printed for the event. I recruited nineteen random strangers in all who are committed to being here to cheer Corey on when she comes. It doesn't hurt that most of them have been drinking and would be up for doing almost anything for twenty bucks apiece.

If she comes.

Merda.

I check my watch. She was supposed to meet me here

five minutes ago. Come on, baby. Just then, a long pair of legs below a red skirt appears on the escalator coming down.

"Here she comes." I clap my hands and the rowdy crew snaps together in a cluster, holding up the sign and waving their flags as the rest of Corey's body comes into view. She's wearing one of the red dresses I bought her and looks like a million bucks. No, a billion. She looks like a winner. Definitely a champion.

"COR-ey, COR-ey, COR-ey," one of the crew starts chanting and the rest join in.

Corey's face comes into view, her hand across her mouth, eyebrows to her hairline. "Oh my god," she mutters as she stumbles off the escalator. I catch her in my arms. "What have you done?"

"I assembled a cheering squad."

Tears swim in her eyes. "Jesus, Stefano," she chokes. "You did this for me? Now you're making me cry." She waves her hands in front of her face, blinking rapidly as she laughs. "I never cry. Only you do this to me."

I slide my hands around her waist and nuzzle her neck. "You're safe with me," I murmur. I'll take her tears. Guard her emotions with my life.

"Thank you," she whispers. "You're amazing." Then she pushes me back and stares at her champions again. "Who *are* these people?" she demands.

I laugh. "Turns out, cheering squads can be hired, which doesn't mean you don't already have raving fans. They just don't know you yet." I wink and steer her toward the door for the competition. "You'd better get in there, it's going to start in ten minutes.

RENEE ROSE

She blows out a quick breath. "Stefano, you're insane."

No, just in love. I don't say it, though. She's too easily scared off and I'm still not certain she feels the same.

"Go in there and kick some ass." I tap her hip because I don't think she'd appreciate having her ass slapped in public.

She squares her shoulders and tosses her gorgeous hair as she marches in to take her seat at the table.

I find a seat in the audience. I only have a view of Corey's back, but the giant screens all around the room televise the event, and the cameras are loving on Corey. Who could blame them? She's about one thousand times easier on the eyes than the grizzled men she's playing against. I'd be surprised if the cameras ever move from her face this entire tournament.

If only she knew how much everyone watching would love to root her on.

~

Corey

I GET DEALT the shittiest cards in the history of poker. I fold three hands in a row. Part of me is ready to just stand up and walk out of here. I've seen enough of gambling to know that when luck isn't with you, you have to walk away.

But Stefano did so much to get me here. Surprised me with this trip, set up the cheering squad. How fucking sweet was that? He actually listened to the story

180

I told him about playing soccer as a kid and tried to remedy it.

He's one in a million, this guy.

And that's why I have to keep playing. Not because he cares whether I win or lose. I believe him when he say he doesn't.

No, I need to win big, because I have a purpose for this money. And it could be a matter of life or death.

I'm not the praying sort, but I start asking Lady Luck, the angels, God, fairies, leprechauns and whatever the hell else might be out there to show up and help me out. And then I remember that desperation never wins. Control wins but not as big or with ease. No, the gut gamblers, they surrender.

So I sit back and imagine I'm tied to Stefano's bed. Imagine I'm surrendering to him. To pleasure. I have no choice but to receive.

A tingling starts between my legs and I have to press my inner thighs together to alleviate the slow throb of my clit. My nipples harden and I start to sweat. All the guys at the table start glancing over at me, like they sense the change.

And I get dealt four aces. Four freaking aces!

And that's when I start to feel the energy pulsing around me. With each hand I win, I get hornier and hornier, as if every win is a sexual gift, every dollar the stimulation I need to get off.

Five hours later, I'm nearly delirious with need and I'm up *one hundred thousand dollars.*

I play it safe until the end of the tournament. When it's finally over, the announcer gives my total winnings and I hear cheers behind me. I spin around and take in the audience. They are whistling and cheering for me. The sound catches on and pretty soon, the entire place is clapping, including the men I was playing with.

Giddiness kicks in and I laugh, disarmed by the unexpected affection of strangers. Fortunately, Stefano appears at my side, because I'm not sure I remember how to walk, and then we're out of there, up to our hotel suite, where he takes me in every position imaginable until I pass out from utter delirium.

CHAPTER 15

 orey

GETTING AWAY from Stefano these days isn't as easy a feat as it should be. I wouldn't call him controlling, but he definitely likes to keep tabs on me.

We flew back today and he went straight to work, but I had to make up a story about meeting a friend for dinner to get him off my back.

I quickly pack the suitcase of cash we brought back into a duffel bag and make the call. In a way, I'm still riding the wave from yesterday. It's like I can see all the possibilities and how they will shape up. I know just how to play each situation. I know just what to say to put Stefano at ease, and I know just what to say to my dad. I keep the call short, urgent and cryptic.

Then I get in my car to meet him.

I don't want to meet at my apartment, but I don't want him anywhere near the Bellissimo either, so it will have to do. The air inside my tiny one-bedroom smells stale, like I haven't lived there in years. Even though it's still my old furniture and my books are on the shelves, it feels nothing like home. I'm not the person I was when I lived here. I don't even like her much. She was closed off, barricaded into a confined existence. Afraid to love, afraid to live.

I take one bundle of cash out of the bag and stash it under the sofa cushion. It doesn't hurt to have a little emergency money.

A knock sounds on the door and my dad pushes it open before I respond. "What's going on? Are you in danger?" His gaze is sharp and he stands up like he's going to try to hug me or something.

Oh that's ripe. Like he ever cared about me. He's just hoping I want to give him the scoop on his case.

"No." I toss the duffel bag filled with my winnings on the couch and unzip it, giving him a nice view of the cash.

"Where did you get that?"

"I won it in a poker tournament."

My dad snorts; he doesn't believe me. That's because he doesn't think I'm good enough to win anything.

"There's a little over one hundred grand in here."

A small smile plays on his lips. He's figured out where this is going. Or he thinks he has. "You want to buy your boyfriend some safety."

I was right.

I always suspected my dad was corrupt. How could anyone who truly believed in justice be such as asshole?

I put my hands on my hips. "That's right."

He nods his head slowly. "All right. I can make his problems go away. But that doesn't mean there won't be new ones. And I may not be the one investigating next time. Is this really the kind of guy you want to keep company with?"

Yeah. I've had this conversation with myself already. It gnaws me up inside. Stefano is a product of his family and he can't get away from them, even if he and his brother are doing their best to rise above it all. So it's absolutely possible there will be another death. More violence. Illegal acts that could endanger Stefano.

But I can't even think about that. I'm just trying to find my way through this crisis, and if I have a way of protecting Stefano, I'm going to do it.

"That's for me to figure out," I say. "Not your problem."

My dad gives a humorless chuckle. "Right." He picks up the bag of cash. "I'll clean up the mess this time. But I suggest you get the hell away from the Tacone family. If I find myself investigating you next time, it won't be so easy for me to suppress evidence."

I want to ask him what evidence he has, just so I know, but I'm itchy to get away from him. I feel dirty and wrong having this conversation and I want it to be over.

"Got it, yeah." I walk to the door and hold it open for him.

He tips an imaginary hat and walks out. "You take care of yourself, Corey Jean."

Fuck you.

I don't say it because he's not worth the breath.

orey

I MAY HAVE BEEN RIDING the wave of luck on my way over, but a growing sense of dread tells me my run is over.

The money's gone, boyfriend saved. I used up my mojo for the moment.

Time to lie low and recharge.

Nothing feels sweet or special anymore. My win in Memphis, Stefano's sweetness, all feel tainted by this exchange.

I drive back, hollowness stretching inside me, threatening to take over, drag me under. I want to go up to Stefano's suite and crawl into bed, pull the covers up over my head and block out life for a few hours. Instead, I stop in Stefano's office to let him know I'm back, or maybe it's because guilt about lying to him is gnawing at me.

Leo's in his office, but Stefano waves me in with a smile. Again, I have that sense of my luck going flat. The buoyancy that swept me through the tournament is dead still. Next time, I'll heed the prickle of warning, the knowing that everything is off. That something's about to go horribly wrong.

As it is, I push away the queasiness, sit down in the chair Stefano waves me into.

"Leo's just showing me a new piece of equipment we got in for security."

"Oh yeah? What is it?"

Leo produces a small wand-type instrument and flips a switch. Green lights illuminate the tip. "It scans for microdevices with signals in them." He stands up and runs it over his own body. It beeps when it goes over his jacket pocket. "You see? That's my cell phone." He produces the phone and sets it on the desk.

He continues waving the wand around, bringing it over my purse, where it turns red and beeps again. "That's your phone."

I unzip my bag and produce the phone, setting it on the desk beside his. He continues scanning my purse and the device beeps again.

"That's weird," I say, digging in my purse again. "What else sets it off?"

Leo and Stefano go dead still. "Bugs." Leo's affable manner's fallen away, his expression icy. "May I?" The words are polite, but the way he says them makes me shiver.

I shove my bag in his direction. Of course I know

there's nothing in it. I glance at Stefano, but he's not looking at me, he's intent on the bag.

Leo waves the wand inside the bag, setting it off again, and he turns the bag inside out. Attached to the lining is a tiny button that makes the device go wild.

Cold flushes through me. "What is that? I've never seen that before." My voice is higher in pitch. I sound like a liar, even to my own ears, but it's the damn truth.

Leo produces a gun and cocks it at my head, the sound loud in the silent office.

I fully expect Stefano to tell him to put it away but he doesn't say a word. His face is pale, expression flat.

Panic surges and I scramble up to my feet. The muzzle of the gun follows me. "I-I didn't know that was in there."

Still keeping the gun trained at my head, Leo advances, waving the wand over me. It doesn't beep again. Stefano picks the bug up and crushes it between his fingers, then he smashes my phone on the side of the desk until it pops open. He examines the inside of it and sets it down.

Tears spear my eyes. "My dad," I choke. "My dad must've put it in there. But I never told him anything. I swear."

"Are you working with your dad?" Stefano's voice is eerily calm and detached.

I shake my head quickly. "No." Tears roll down my face. "But he's here in Las Vegas. He's investigating the disappearance of Donahue. I told him I didn't know anything, but maybe that's when he—" I swipe at my tears with the back of my hand. "When he put it in there."

Jesus, my story sounds stupid and implausible even though it's the stone cold truth.

"When was this?" Stefano clips.

"Right after it happened." My voice cracks. "He was at my apartment when I came home."

"And you kept that from me." Stefano says it like I've just forever damned myself.

"He was in Chicago, too." I admit, as if telling him now will make up for my earlier omissions. "At the wedding. He said he has evidence. I gave him the money from Memphis to suppress it."

Stefano surges to his feet, knocking his chair to the floor. I don't move, even though I'm shaking like a baby bird. He fists my hair and brings his face close to mine.. A muscle tics in his cheek, but his eyes are dead. "You tell your father," he snarls, "he shouldn't get his family involved in business."

It's a bald threat and I'm full-on terrified. It's a wonder I don't piss myself.

"You broke my fucking heart, Corey Simonson."

I squeeze my eyes shut, because his expression is breaking mine, but he releases me abruptly and shoves me away. "Get out. Don't ever come back here. Don't ever let me see your face again, *bella*. I won't show mercy a second time."

"Stefano," I whisper-plead. I want to explain—or better yet, go back in time and be more transparent from the beginning. Maybe I could avoid this betrayal of his faith in me.

But it's too late. Leo grabs my elbow and yanks me through the door, slamming it behind me.

I can barely see as I toddle out, tears blinding me. My purse is still in their office, so I have nothing: no keys, no money, no phone, nowhere to go.

I find my way outside and start walking, away from the Bellissimo, away from Stefano. Away from everything I loved.

Stefano

THE MINUTE SHE'S GONE, I throw the desk over. I want to smash everything in sight. She never loved me. She played me. Ruined me.

Leo watches, silent at first. "Want me to take care of her?"

"No."

Even as angry as I am, as broken and betrayed and fucking *insane* as I am, I could never harm Corey.

"I'm not sure you really have the perspective necessary to make this call."

I throw myself at Leo, cut off his air as I shove him up against the wall. "You don't *ever* question my judgment. Not on this. Not on anything. *Capiche?*"

"Yeah. Got it, boss," Leo says quickly.

I storm out, because if I stay, I'm going to kill the guy. I go up to our suite—*my* suite—*fuck!*—and I immediately know it was a mistake.

The place smells like her. Reminds me of her. Slays me.

I go on a rampage, throwing furniture, putting my fist through the wall.

All this fucking time I thought she was holding back because she was protecting her heart. But she wasn't. She was playing me.

I heard the warning bells about her fucking dad. I knew getting involved with her would bite me. I just chose to ignore it. I was too captivated by the enigma that is Corey Simonson. I wanted to be the guy who set her free. Wanted to know what it's like to get inside her shell. To be her man.

I am a fucking idiot.

I pace around the wrecked room, trying to remember every single thing I ever said in her presence. She saw me shoot Donahue. That's a problem, for sure. But what else—

I stop.

She saw me shoot Donahue and didn't go to the cops. If she had, why would they need a bug? Unless they want to take down Nico, too. Or just get as much info as possible.

I rub my bruised knuckles.

What if she told me the truth? Her dad planted it on her after the shooting. She didn't tell him anything. He's digging, using his in, but he has nothing.

Because Corey wouldn't betray me.

Hot emotion chokes me. My eyes burn.

Fuck! I slam my fist into the wall again.

I don't know what to believe.

Was Leo right? Is my judgment too off on this one to know what's happening?

Or did I just make the biggest mistake of my life?

Corey

I DON'T KNOW how long I walk—until my feet are blistered and my calves are in spasm. I somehow end up back at the Bellissimo—precisely where I'm not supposed to be. I take the elevator to the top deck of the parking lot and look over the edge.

No, I'm not thinking about jumping. I'm not stupid or suicidal. And while the pain in my chest is startling, I have a lot more to worry about right now than a broken heart. I need to worry about my immediate survival.

I am so fucked right now.

I think it's quite possible someone will come after me, despite the fact that Stefano let me go. Which means going to my place would be a mistake.

I could contact Sondra. I know she'd do anything in the world for me, but if Nico or any of his soldiers want to find me, she's going to be the first person they look to for answers. I don't want to put her in that position.

I do have the stash of money under my couch cushion. I need to get there and get it out without anyone seeing me.

I head back out to the strip and hail a cab. It's not a great plan, but it's a start. Once I have a place to stay I can contemplate what I've lost.

Stefano.

The only man who ever saw the real me.

CHAPTER 17

 tefano

"Any sign of her?" I bark in my phone to Leo. I have him sitting in front of Corey's apartment, in hopes she'll show up. It's been twenty hours since I threw her out and I'm going out of my fucking mind.

It took me the first six hours to pull my head out of my ass and realize Corey might not have been playing me. In retrospect, it seems obvious. Would she have just let Leo scan her purse without batting an eyelash if she'd been hiding something? If she knew she was carrying a bug? I've been looking for her ever since.

"No, none. No sign of life here at all."

Fanculo.

The fact that her car's still sitting in the Bellissimo lot and she's not at her apartment absolutely guts me.

It means she's hiding. She's afraid.

Of me.

Because I'm the *stronzo* who tossed her out and told her to never show her face again like a fucking idiot. So much for *I will always defend you*. I let my fear of not being good enough, of a fed's daughter never being able to be with a guy like me create some monstrous betrayal in my head instead of just taking the time to *listen* to her. She doesn't even have a phone, or her wallet.

If it's true she gave the money from Memphis to her father, she has nothing.

Maybe she went to him.

It's an uneasy thought. Would he take care of her? The man who put a bug in his own daughter's purse, putting her life in jeopardy?

I need answers. I need fucking information. I head up to Sondra's office and barge in. Nico's in with her, sitting on her desk.

"Where's your cousin?" I demand.

She stands up, her blue eyes round. "What do you mean?"

I stalk around toward her, but Nico blocks my way. "Take a fucking step back," he warns. "What's going on?"

"Corey. Have you heard from her? At all?"

Sondra's brows pinch. "No. What happened? Did you have a fight?"

I stab my fingers through my hair. "You could say that." I turn and look out the floor to ceiling windows. "Tell me about her dad."

Sondra draws in a sharp breath. "He's an asshole," she says without hesitation. "I can't tell you how many nights she spent as a kid at my house because she didn't want to go home."

My chest tightens.

"Corey hasn't talked to him in years."

"You sure about that? He was or is here, in Vegas." I watch her closely.

Her expression sours like something smells bad in the room. "He was?"

"And in Chicago."

Fear flickers over Sondra's face and Nico curses. "What the fuck are you talking about?"

"He dropped a bug in Corey's purse. She says she paid him off to drop his investigation of me."

Sondra covers her mouth with her hand. "Oh no. So where is she? What happened?"

I pace around the room. "I fucked up." I jab an angry hand into the air. "I threw her out. I didn't know what to believe."

"Oh no," Sondra says again.

"Now she's missing. I have her purse and keys. She's not at her place. Her car's still in the lot. I don't know where the fuck she went or how to get ahold of her."

"How long has she been gone?"

"Since yesterday. Any ideas of where she would go? What she would do?"

Sondra's eyes well with tears. "No. She should've called me."

My phone rings and I pull it out. It's a Michigan number. I answer. "Tacone speaking."

"Special Agent Simonson, FBI."

I tense up, motion my brother over.

"I believe you're aware I'm investigating you."

I grunt an affirmative. My hand tightens so hard on the phone I fear it will crack.

"I'm willing to discuss dropping the investigation."

I am going to kill this man.

No wait, I can't. He's still Corey's fucking father.

"What are your terms?" I don't bother arguing that he already took money from Corey to drop it if her story is true, which I'm coming to believe it is.

"Five hundred grand in cash and I destroy the evidence. Deliver it at 8:00 p.m. tonight in the parking garage of the Hard Rock Cafe."

He ends the call without waiting for my answer.

"What evidence?" Nico snaps.

I shake my head. "It's a bluff. Unless Corey's working with him."

"Corey's *not* working with him," Sondra cries, fingers balled into fists. "How could you even think that?"

I drop my chin to my chest in defeat. "I don't. I really don't. Would she go to him for help?" I ask Sondra. "Do you think she's with him?"

"No way—never. I'm telling you, she's not even on speaking terms with him."

"So what's the play?" Nico asks.

"I meet him. Find out if he knows where Corey is."

"Then what?" Nico wants to know.

I shrug. No fucking clue. "I'll figure it the fuck out."

"Take Leo and Eddie. Are you bringing the cash?"

"No." My voice is harder than stone. No fucking way I'm giving that man more money. He already robbed Corey of hers and he still thinks he can blackmail me?

Fuck him. Dirty feds stink worse than the lowest of the underground.

"Good."

Yeah good. But I'm still no closer to finding Corey. "Sondra, if Corey calls you…" I break off and rub my sternum because I don't know what the fuck to say. Even if I tell Corey I believe her, is she really going to come back here with me?

After the way I treated her? Threatened her life?

She's a smart, self-respecting woman. If she's not in trouble right now, then she's already as far from here as she can get.

The thing that kills me is that she might be in trouble. I left her with very few options.

And I know hundreds of unspeakable things that happen to women who run out of options in Vegas.

"If I hear from her, I'll tell her you fucked up and you really want to apologize," Sondra fills in.

I throw her a grateful look.

"Yeah, exactly. Thanks."

Sondra's eyes look haunted, though, and she can't even be half as worried about Corey as I am.

Madonna help me.

Corey

It's four in the afternoon and I'm still in the nasty motel bed. It's not like I've slept. Well, maybe I drowsed a little, but every time I do, I dream of Stefano getting shot. Or shooting me.

I wake up with a pain in my chest like it really happened.

How did things get so messed up? How can I make it right?

I simply can't allow Stefano to believe I used him. Why did I never tell him how much he meant to me? That he's the only guy I've ever fallen for? How much I appreciate—no, appreciate isn't deep enough—how he devastated me with his thoughtfulness. His love. I know he never said it, but only love would make a man work so hard to lift his woman's belief in herself. If only I'd done something to show him my love, too. Then he wouldn't have doubted me. Wouldn't have believed I could betray him.

I stumble out of bed and take a shower in the dingy bathroom.

What's my plan?

I need a plan. Finding out where I really stand with the Tacones would be a start. I need to call Sondra. And maybe she can help me figure out a way to prove to Stefano I wasn't a part of my father's plan.

I put on my dirty clothes and walk to a Walgreens on the corner where I buy a pair of flip flops, leggings and a t-shirt so I at least have something to change into. I also get a burner phone to make calls.

I hardly have anyone's number memorized anymore, but Sondra and I have been close since before the dawn of cell phones. I still know her number by heart. I dial it, my nerves jangling as I wait for her to pick up.

"Hello?"

"Hey, it's me."

"Corey, thank God! Where are you? Where have you been? Stefano is looking for you."

"I was afraid of that. My dad—"

"Stefano told me about the bug and that you tried to pay your dad off. He's already called Stefano to blackmail him for more."

"What?"

Of all the possible scenarios, that one hadn't crossed my mind.

"Yeah, Stefano's meeting him tonight in the Hard Rock parking garage."

My heart thuds painfully against my chest. This is exactly what I need—my dad and Stefano in the same room—or garage, as the case may be. A chance to prove to Stefano I'm not a part of my dad's nasty schemes.

"Thanks, that's what I need to know," I say.

"Wait, Corey!" Sondra yelps into the phone to stop me from hanging up. "Where are you? What are you going to do?"

"I'm going to prove to Stefano I wasn't a part of this shitstorm. Or at least make him believe I didn't know I was bugged. I should've told him about my dad investigating him—that's on me. But I had no idea my dad planted a bug."

"Stefano's worried about you."

My chest constricts painfully.

He still cares.

I can fix this.

I can't speak because my throat clogs with tears. "Thanks, Sondra. I'll be in touch."

CHAPTER 18

 *tefano*

I'M ready to chew up and spit out everyone around me. I need to get a grip on my aggression or I'm going to smash in Corey's dad's skull. I hope to fuck he knows where she is.

We put on kevlar vests under our shirts because I definitely don't trust this guy. All three of us also set our phones to record. Audio surveillance goes both ways. Having evidence against Mr. Crooked Fed could be useful.

I didn't like what Sondra said about Corey's childhood with this dickbag. I already knew it sucked, but now I want to make him pay for it. He damaged her. I want him to bleed.

Dial it back, stronzo.

We arrive at the Hard Rock and pull into the underground parking area. I get out with the suitcase full of nothing and we check our weapons. There are video cameras up in the corners, but it looks to me like someone already shot them out.

Okay, dickhead. Where are you?

I stroll through the garage like I'm going for a goddamn walk with my dog through the tulips until I spot him, leaning up against a pillar.

"Simonson."

"Tacone."

"Where's your daughter?"

"She's somewhere safe," he says, simultaneously relieving me and ripping my heart out. She did go to him for help.

Is she working with him?

Fuck—I know she's not. *She's not.*

"She's ready and willing to testify against you, but she doesn't want to."

My heart slows, drags like a lame horse in my chest.

"Oh yeah?" Now I'm just teenage bluster. I can't even think. Can't discern what's what here. Dammit. Corey *is* my blind spot. I should've let Nico or Leo take the lead on this.

"That's bullshit!"

I nearly drop to my knees.

Corey comes marching out from around the corner, looking like a fiery angel with her red hair spilling out behind her.

"Corey, get back," her father barks, but she ignores him. She's blazing toward *me*. Anger crackles all around her and my heart skips up to speed. I'm suddenly sure of her—I know this woman.

Fury crosses her father's face. I should've paid attention, but I only have eyes for Corey. I need to apologize, let her know I believe her.

"Stefano, I'm not a part of his scheme. Not at all. Don't believe a word he says."

"Stefano," Leo barks, drawing his weapon.

It's too late. Simonson fires on Leo, hitting him in the chest.

Corey whirls. "No!" she screams and leaps in front of me. Her body jerks and crumples to the asphalt.

I draw my pistol and fire on Simonson. The bullet hits him right in the forehead but I don't wait to see him fall, I'm running for Corey. "Call 911," I shout at my men, scooping her into my arms. Blood spreads rapidly across the top of her shirt. I ball it up and push on the wound.

No, please.

Don't let her die.

Not now. Not like this.

How could I have doubted her love?

She took a goddamn bullet for me.

And I failed her.

In every possible way.

CHAPTER 19

 orey

My throat kills me, eyes feel gritty. The astringent smell of disinfectant hits my nose before I manage to crack my lids.

Oh God. I'm alive. I'm alive and Stefano thinks I betrayed him. I blink, trying to focus as my eyes adjust to being open.

A face comes into view, but it's not the one I want to see—the one I *need* to see. "Stefano?" I manage to croak through dry lips.

Sondra surges off the chair beside me, leans over. "She's awake!"

"What…" I lick my lips. "Where is Stefano?"

"Get out."

My heart surges at the harsh, clipped sound of his voice. He's alive. Free. Here.

But he sounds angry.

"Watch how you talk to my wife." It takes me a moment to place the angry growl before the figure of Nico looms into view.

"Will you *please* both get out?" Stefano's normal easy-going charm is completely absent.

"You're lucky I know what it's like to be in your shoes with your balls hanging in the wind," Nico remarks.

"Fuck off and get out." Stefano looks like shit. His jaw is shadowed, expression haggard.

"I'll be back," Sondra promises me, but I hardly spare her a glance. I can't look away from Stefano's intense gaze, which is locked on my face.

"Stefano." My voice is so hoarse I can hardly speak, but I have to get this out. I push myself up to sit and swing my legs over the edge of the hospital bed. Pain shoots down my left arm and I gasp.

"Back in bed, back in bed." Stefano lurches to my side and scoops my legs back up onto the mattress. "What are you doing?"

"Stefano, I didn't know about the bug—"

"Shh." He puts his finger on my lips. "I know, *bella*. I know. I shouldn't have doubted you. I'm so fucking sorry." He pulls up the chair Sondra occupied and sits beside me, holding my hand. An IV is attached to my arm.

I rub my dry lips together. "Thirsty."

Stefano jumps up and retrieves a water bottle, which he holds to my lips. I drink, liquid dribbling down my chin onto the thin hospital gown.

There's suddenly too much to say and no words to say it. I stare up at Stefano, at a loss. "Are you still mad at me?" It's all I can think to ask. It's the only thing that really matters to me right now.

His brow furrows. "Hell yes, I'm mad."

My heart plummets.

"Don't you ever—*ever*—take a bullet for me again. I can take care of myself. *Capiche?*"

Tears spring to my eyes as I remember the moment of horror I experienced when I thought he would die.

"Hey." He brushes my cheek with the back of his fingers. *"Perdonami.* Corey, I have to tell you something." He looks around the room like it will supply him with strength. "It's bad."

The tears well up again, even though I don't know what he's going to say.

"I know we have a lot to talk about. I don't even know if you would've forgiven me for what I did to you—how I acted. But I've done something even worse."

The anticipation makes it so much worse. Or maybe it's the pain. I can't stop the tears from spilling from my eyes, even though I don't know what he's going to say.

"Your father's dead. I killed him."

Oh.

I blink the remaining tears back.

"Okay."

He lifts a brow. "Okay? Did you hear me?"

"I heard you," I croak, my raw throat grating. "He killed Leo. He almost killed me." I touch the bandage above my heart. "Of course you shot him."

Stefano strokes my hair back from my face, cups my

cheek, concern etched into his features. "Leo's not dead; we were wearing Kevlar. The doctor says you're going to pull through. You'll need physical therapy for your shoulder, but it should mend." He picks up my hand and brings my fingers to his lips, kissing them. "Corey, say you'll forgive me. For your father. For throwing you out. I messed up. Big time. But I'll never doubt you again, I promise. And if you give me another chance, I swear I'll work my ass off to make it all up to you. I'll spend the rest of my life trying."

"I love you, Stefano," I blurt, my cheeks wet with tears.

For a second there, I swear I see moisture in Stefano's eyes, too, but then my tough guy blinks them back. "Baby, I love you, too. I'm fucking crazy about you. Say you'll come back with me when they let you out of here."

I nod through my tears. "Yes, of course. That's where I want to go." I sniff. "You're the only one who ever saw the real me."

Stefano grows serious, picking up both my hands. "I want to discover everything there is to know about you."

"I'm sorry I held back. I was a coward. My fear of getting hurt is exactly what got me hurt." I give a watery laugh. "Ironic, huh?"

"I'll never hurt you again," Stefano swears.

I squeeze his hands. "What happened with my dad? What did the police do?"

"Your dad turned up dead in an alley in Detroit where he was working a case."

"He was still working in Detroit? He told me he'd been transferred here."

Stefano shakes his head. "No, he lied about that, too.

He was here on personal time, looking for ways to manipulate his daughter's situation to make money. Your winnings from Memphis have been recovered, by the way. The police will want to talk to you about the purse snatcher who shot you in the Hard Rock parking lot just before we found you. I imagine they'll be in as soon as they hear you're awake."

"Got it." I reach for the water bottle and drink some more down. I'm not even worried about talking to the police. I don't question Stefano's methods.

Justice was served, in its own way. It doesn't matter to me if it happened on the right or wrong side of the law. My father didn't uphold those laws.

"A little bit of good news? Turns out your dad never took your mom off his life insurance as beneficiary. She'll be getting a quarter million as soon as things are settled."

I smile. Yep. Justice has definitely been served. My mom deserves that money after putting up with my asswipe of a dad for all those years before he left.

She can retire from her job as a school attendance clerk, figure out how to make herself happy.

Me—I already know what makes me happy, and he's sitting right in front of me.

EPILOGUE

S *tefano*

"You can't keep me a prisoner in here forever," Corey protests from where I have her tied to the bed.

"Mmm, isn't this how our relationship started?" I work the knot on the silk tie securing her open and scoop her up into my arms. I've kept her prisoner in our suite since she returned home from the hospital two days ago. The doctors said she needed to rest and let her wound recover fully before she begins any activity and she hasn't received the green light yet.

"I am capable of walking," she protests as I carry her into the living room and settle her on the couch.

"No more TV," she groans. "I'm bored. You can't leave me alone here any longer. I'm going nuts."

"I'm not leaving you. Nico's got things covered tonight. I'm staying in with you."

Her stubborn expression melts away, and the softness and affection replacing it takes my breath. She's been showing me glimpses of this side of her since the hospital, and every time, it humbles me to my core.

I drag an end table in front of her and get a chair for me. "How about a game of cards?" I suggest, shuffling the deck.

She scoffs. "Are you serious?"

"Mmm hmm. We'll bet clothing. Or"—I shoot her a wicked look—"sexual acts."

Her lips twist. "You won't let me walk from the bedroom to the living room, but you think I'm ready to suck your dick?"

I wink. "I'm sure we can find something that works for you."

She grins and takes the cards out of my hand. "You're on, buddy. You know you're the one who's going to find himself on his knees, right?"

I'm counting on it, amore.

She shuffles the deck and deals the first hand, which I promptly lose.

"So you wanted me on my knees?" I slide out of my chair and drop to my knees in front of her, pushing her thighs open. She's in nothing but a short silk robe and a pair of panties. I run my fingertips up her inner thighs and she shivers.

"Stefano." Her voice wobbles when I nip her inner thigh with my teeth. "I really don't know if I'm for it. "I mean, I want it, but I'm afraid I'll get too excited and—"

"Well, there's other things to do on my knees," I rumble, reaching in my pocket.

She watches me with a quizzical look until I produce a small ring box and pop it open. She gasps and covers her mouth with her hand. "Stefano."

"I know you don't like to rush into things, but there's no way in hell I'm going to let you take a bullet for me without putting a ring on that finger," I say in the world's stupidest proposal speech. I clear my throat. "What I mean is… *stay,* baby. Stay forever. I need you by my side, lighting up my world. I know we don't have our future figured out, but I want to figure mine out with you. I want to be a part of yours." Fuck. I don't know where I'm going with this speech. Are there issues I need to address? Or do I just ask her to marry me?

"Yes."

It's like plunging into warm water. "Did you say yes?"

"Yes." She laughs, tears glistening in her eyes. "I'm done playing small, playing safe. We don't have time *not* to rush into this. We have our lives to start living—together."

"Yeah?" I laugh. "You're gonna wear my ring?"

She plucks the pink diamond from the box and slides it on her left ring finger. "I'm wearing it." She holds her hand up to show me and I kiss her palm.

"Good. Now I'm going to assert my manly rights." I kiss the inside of her leg.

Her fingers weave into my hair. "Stefano."

"I'll go easy on you just this once." I wink before I shove her panties to the side and lick into her.

The End

I HOPE you enjoyed *Jack of Spades*. If you loved it, please consider reviewing it or recommending to a friend—your reviews help indie authors so much.

Want more Vegas Underground? You can pre-order the next book in the series, *Ace of Hearts!* Read a taster of Tony's story on the next page!

Also check out the first book in *Vegas Underground* series, **King of Diamonds** and the bonus story, **Mafia Daddy (included in the anthology Daddy's Demands).**

Don't miss any releases! Sign up for my mailing list: http://owned.gr8.com. Are you in my super private Facebook group **Renee's Romper Room**? If not, send me an email at renee@reneeroseromance.com to request membership with the email you use to login to Facebook.

WANT MORE? A TEASER FROM ACE OF HEARTS

Ace of Hearts: **A Mafia Romance**
Vegas Underground, Book Three

The songbird trapped in a cage.

My manager made a deal with the devil
and now his right hand man has come to collect.
I owe millions to the mob, which means
The hulking Tony Brando now owns me.

I'll be headlining at his boss' casino until the debt
is paid.

Unless he decides to keep me forever.

Chapter One

Pepper

The limo pulls up at the Bellissimo and a bellhop opens the door for me.

You know your career's reached a new low when you're booked for three weeks in Vegas.

I don't care if the Bellissimo is the swankiest, hippest place in Sin City, it's still Vegas. The shithole performers go to for low stress, easy money. Usually after they're burned out.

So why the hell am I here twenty months after the release of an album and less than fourteen hours after the last performance of a grueling tour?

Because Hugh, my asshole manager, sold me out.

And now my parents, Hugh and I are in a world of trouble only I can fix.

Anton, my bodyguard, gets out first, then offers a hand to help me. I ignore it, because, yeah, I'm twenty-three, so fully capable of getting out of a car on my own, and not prissy enough to want help, although I appreciate the gesture. I climb out and shake down the skirt of my strappy, babydoll dress, which I paired with a beat up pair of brick red Doc Martens, and pop my earbuds out, the Radiohead album still playing.

A forty-something woman in a blue dress and heels clips out of the door, making a beeline for Hugh. Behind her, a huge, broad-shouldered man stands just outside the gold-trimmed door watching.

Watching *me*.

That's not unusual. I'm the popstar, after all, but it's the way he watches that sends rockets of warning shooting through my veins. His unimpressed, quiet observation and fine Italian suit give him away.

He's Tony Brando, the man who now owns me.

I recognize him. He showed up to my concert in Vancouver, and again in Denver.

He's the reason we're here, despite the fact that I'm three hours from a total collapse, about to lose my voice and in desperate need of some alone time.

Of course, even if the mob wasn't after me for millions of dollars, Hugh probably would still have me booked until the next century. My well-being never factored into his or my parents' plans for my career.

I told Hugh two years ago I needed a break. Time to find my muse again and make the music that catapulted me into stardom in the first place. I wanted to hole up in a studio to record my next album, which would fix the cash flow problem my parents were in after some bad investments last year.

But Hugh had a scheme.

An idiotic, dangerous plan that my parents and I blindly trusted him to execute.

"Welcome, Ms. Heart. I'm Angela Torrino, Director of Events. The Bellissimo is so thrilled to have you, as you can see." She gestures to the hundred-foot neon sign out on the strip with my name in lights.

I shake her hand and try to force a smile. Try not to glance at the pinstriped suit lurking behind her.

Hugh trots around and takes over, as always. "Thanks for making the arrangements, Ms. Torrino." He pumps her hand. "Now, if you can get us access to the stage, we'll start loading in so Pepper can rehearse before her performance tonight."

Right. Rehearse—now. Because lord knows it's a sacrilege to actually have one day of rest after traveling before I perform. Or even an hour.

I follow Hugh and Ms. Torrino toward the hotel/casino doors, Anton right behind me and slightly to my left.

Ms. Torrino stops to introduce Hugh to the large man in the doorway. Brando ignores her and steps forward. His movements are graceful for a man at least six and a half feet tall and over 250 pounds. His gaze is clearly on my face, and not in the *wow-I'm-meeting-the-famous-young-rockstar-Pepper-Heart* way. No, it's more a big bad wolf surveying his prey.

His gaze skims over my face to my braless breasts and on down my bare legs. Then back up again at a more leisurely pace, resting on my eyes.

I'm pretty sure he likes what he sees, but he doesn't leer. The smirk on his mouth is more one of satisfaction, like I'm a fine wine that's just been delivered to him and he's savoring my scent.

My stomach knots.

"Ms. Heart, this is Antonio Brando, one of the Directors of Operations here at the Bellissimo," Ms. Torrino chirps from behind him. I'd like to say his big scary visage makes him ugly, but it would be a lie. Even with the light lines of scars marring his rugged jaw, forehead, and left cheek, he's beautiful. Like some sort of Roman demi-god sent to Earth to rip apart men and conquer women until the lowly humans have all been tamed.

He doesn't offer his hand. I don't either. In fact, I give him my best *fuck you* stare—the one I usually reserve for Hugh.

"I'm looking forward to your show tonight." His baritone moves through me, vibrating right between my thighs.

I really wish my body didn't have this reaction to his closeness, because I'd much rather hate the man than be turned on by him. But he's massive masculine power; he radiates quiet confidence and control. And menace. Yes, there's an undercurrent of violence to him that sends shivers running down my spine.

I clamp my lips together because I can't think of anything to say that won't get my kneecaps broken. And I'm pretty sure that happens here. The Bellissimo is owned and run by the Tacone crime family. Besides, and more importantly, I don't want him to hear the state of my voice. It's almost gone. I've been sick for weeks now and I honestly don't know if I can make it through this last stint in Vegas.

Hugh bustles to my side and grabs my elbow in that controlling way of his. "Come on, let's get you to that stage so you can rehearse. I want no flub-ups tonight."

I put my head down and follow, not because I agree that I need the rehearsal time, but because I need to get away from Brando's searing regard. As fast as possible.

Hugh's grip tightens on my elbow as we move through the casino. "Do you want to get us all killed?" he hisses in my ear, his breath stinking of sour coffee.

"I thought you already took care of that." I use my most dry, bored tone—the one that sets him off on a rampage. Then I tune out the lecture as Bellissimo guests call out my name and start snapping photos. I grin and flash them the peace sign as we walk through casino on a long parade from the front door to the concert hall where my tour bus is parked in the way back. Of course we could've just pulled around there to begin with, but this is Hugh's strategy of making sure everyone knows there's someone famous in the building—hyping the show.

A group of rowdy frat boys jostle too close, getting into my space to snag selfies with me. Anton barks for them to back up, shielding my body with his, but suddenly casino security swarm around us, forming a protective bubble.

"I don't know, she only has one bodyguard," one of them speaks into a comms unit, then, "You got it, Tony. We'll stay with her at all times."

Tony.

I twist around to see my huge keeper. He's walking casually behind us, his lips moving as he gives orders to his staff. Our gazes meet and lock, his dark, promising.

My heart picks up speed.

I want to march back and say all the things I bit back when we met outside, but it's like the Earth is rumbling beneath my feet. The tetonic plates shifting and moving, rearranging.

I may have thought I could handle Vegas. Handle my obligations at the Bellissimo. Get in, get out, hold my breakdown until it's over. But now that I've met Tony Brando, I know I'm in way over my head.

It's hard to imagine I'll survive this gig with my soul intact.

PRE-ORDER NOW!

WANT FREE RENEE ROSE BOOKS?

Click here to sign up for Renee Rose's newsletter and receive a free copy of *Theirs to Protect, Owned by the Marine, Theirs to Punish, The Alpha's Punishment, Disobedience at the Dressmaker's* and *Her Billionaire Boss.* In addition to the free stories, you will also get special pricing, exclusive previews and news of new releases.

ABOUT RENEE ROSE

USA TODAY BESTSELLING AUTHOR RENEE ROSE is a naughty wordsmith who writes kinky romance novels. Named Eroticon USA's Next Top Erotic Author in 2013, she has also won *Spunky and Sassy's* Favorite Sci-Fi and Anthology Author, *The Romance Reviews* Best Historical Romance, and *Spanking Romance Reviews'* Best Historical, Best Erotic, Best Ageplay and favorite author. She's hit #1 on Amazon in the Erotic Paranormal, Western and Sci-fi categories. She also pens BDSM stories under the name Darling Adams.

Please follow her on:
   Bookbub | **Goodreads** | **Instagram**

Renee loves to connect with readers!
www.reneeroseromance.com
reneeroseauthor@gmail.com

OTHER TITLES BY RENEE ROSE

Vegas Underground Mafia Romance

King of Diamonds

Jack of Spades

Ace of Hearts (pre-order now, coming Dec 1st)

Mafia Daddy (in Daddy's Demands)

More Mafia Romance

The Russian

The Don's Daughter

Mob Mistress

The Bossman

Contemporary

Blaze: A Firefighter Daddy Romance

Black Light: Roulette Redux

Her Royal Master

The Russian

Black Light: Valentine Roulette

Theirs to Protect

Scoring with Santa

Owned by the Marine

Theirs to Punish

Punishing Portia

The Professor's Girl

Safe in his Arms

Saved

The Elusive "O"

Paranormal

Bad Boy Alphas Series

Alpha's Bane (coming Nov. 1st)

Alpha's Mission

Alpha's War

Alpha's Desire

Alpha's Obsession

Alpha's Challenge

Alpha's Prize

Alpha's Danger

Alpha's Temptation

Love in the Elevator (Bonus story to Alpha's Temptation)

Alpha Doms Series

The Alpha's Hunger

The Alpha's Promise

The Alpha's Punishment

Other Paranormals

His Captive Mortal

Deathless Love

Deathless Discipline

The Winter Storm: An Ever After Chronicle

Sci-Fi

Zandian Masters Series

His Human Slave

His Human Prisoner

Training His Human

His Human Rebel

His Human Vessel

His Mate and Master

Zandian Pet

Their Zandian Mate

His Human Possession

Zandian Brides (Reverse Harem)

Night of the Zandians

Bought by the Zandians

The Hand of Vengeance

Her Alien Masters

Regency

The Darlington Incident

Humbled

The Reddington Scandal

The Westerfield Affair

Pleasing the Colonel

Western

His Little Lapis

The Devil of Whiskey Row

The Outlaw's Bride

Medieval

Mercenary

Medieval Discipline

Lords and Ladies

The Knight's Prisoner

Betrothed

Held for Ransom

The Knight's Seduction

The Conquered Brides (5 book box set)

Renaissance

Renaissance Discipline

Ageplay

Stepbrother's Rules

Her Hollywood Daddy

His Little Lapis

Black Light: Valentine's Roulette (Broken)

BDSM under the name Darling Adams

Made in the USA
Coppell, TX
14 March 2021